PUFFIN CLASSICS

The Burmese Box

D0836140

The Burmese Box
Two Novellas

LILA MAJUMDAR

Translated from the Bengali by Srilata Banerjee

Introduction by Subhadra Sen Gupta

PUFFIN BOOKS

PUFFIN BOOKS

Published by the Penguin Group

Penguin Books India Pvt. Ltd, 11 Community Centre, Panchsheel Park, New Delhi 110 017, India

Penguin Group (USA) Inc., 375 Hudson Street, New York, New York 10014, USA

Penguin Group (Canada), 90 Eglinton Avenue East, Suite 700, Toronto, Ontario, M4P 2Y3, Canada (a division of Pearson Penguin Canada Inc.)

Penguin Books Ltd, 80 Strand, London WC2R 0RL, England

Penguin Ireland, 25 St Stephen's Green, Dublin 2, Ireland (a division of Penguin Books Ltd)

Penguin Group (Australia), 707 Collins Street, Melbourne, Victoria 3008, Australia (a division of Pearson Australia Group Pty Ltd)

Penguin Group (NZ), 67 Apollo Drive, Rosedale, Auckland 0632, New Zealand (a division of Pearson New Zealand Ltd)

Penguin Group (South Africa) (Pty) Ltd, Block D, Rosebank Office Park, 181 Jan Smuts Avenue, Parktown North, Johannesburg 2193, South Africa

Penguin Books Ltd, Registered Offices: 80 Strand, London WC2R 0RL, England

First published in Puffin by Penguin Books India 2010

Text copyright © The Estate of Lila Majumdar 2010
Translation copyright © Srilata Banerjee 2010

10 9 8 7 6 5 4 3 2

ISBN 9780143331483

Typeset in Minion by Eleven Arts, New Delhi
Printed at Repro India Ltd., Navi Mumbai

Contents

Introduction

Adults never *get* it, do they? I mean, how many adults do you know who understand what it is like to be eleven and a half years old and running out of chewing gum?

They can't remember what they had for breakfast and you think they can recall what it was like to be four-and-a-half feet tall and not being able to reach the top shelf of the cupboard where your grandma had hidden the box of pickles?

Some hope.

Well, there was one adult who *always* got it. And the amazing thing is that she understood the great problems of growing up even when she was really *quite old* . . . you know like thirty-eight or something . . .

This was a writer named Lila Majumdar, and I absolutely and utterly adored her books. I fell in love with them when I was eleven and a half, and I still adore them. They are the most battered books in my bookcase and you can still discover ancient bits of potato chips in between the pages. As a kid I loved her books because Lila Majumdar could enter my head, sort of peer around and say, 'Hmmm . . . hate Maths, do ya? Flunked in Hindi again? And your angelic kid sister has cute dimples and can sing Rabindra Sangeet and you hate her?' I was convinced she could read my mind.

Lila Majumdar was a *genius*. There was only one problem

with her books and that was they were written in Bengali and so only lucky kids (like me), who could read that language, could open their hearts and minds to her.

Luckily for all of you, she has a granddaughter named Srilata Banerjee and oh joy! She has translated her grandma's stories into English, so that my absolutely number one writer for kids can be read by all of you. Now that is what I call a *good* granddaughter; bless her and may she translate more. And if I could make a few suggestions . . . there is a book called *Tong Ling* (my copy is held together with green electrical tape) and a short story collection called *Bagher Chokh* (in my copy page 42 is missing) could she do them next please?

When I was growing up there was a totally cool kid's magazine called *Sandesh*. I discovered Lila Majumdar in the pages of *Sandesh* and very often her stories were illustrated by this gentleman called Satyajit Ray. That's right guys, the world famous film director! Lila Majumdar was his aunt and the two of them edited the magazine. Satyajit Ray wrote and illustrated the stories about a detective called Feluda and they were great. Lila Majumdar wrote about Goopy and Panchu Mama, Podi-pishi and Thandidi, Birinchi-da and a strange thin man in a lungi and suspiciously oiled curly hair. And I have to admit, Goopy and Podi-pishi were even more interesting. These stories were full of crazy happenings and weird surprises and such great fun.

Now, I have a cousin who, when he was eleven and a half, liked to read under the bed. It was mainly for some peace and quiet and because adults can't crawl under beds, so they can't get there and force you to brush your teeth. My grandma had this high, four-poster bed and on hot summer holiday afternoons he would crawl under it with a handful of biscuits and vanish into the world of *Sandesh*. If he was feeling kind he would let me join him and we would lie on our stomachs on the cool mosaic floor and read. Occasionally Grandma would peer down and ask, 'Why are you laughing?' and it was because we were reading . . . you know who . . .

When you read 'The Burmese Box' you'll discover Panchu Mama disappearing under a four-poster bed. Now how did Lila Majumdar know that kids like the underside of beds? Because she must have done the same as a kid and she *remembered*. That was the magic of her stories.

Also, she always *understood*. She understood what it felt like to look at a tiffin-carrier full of aloo-puri, mutton cutlets and sweet sohan papri and feel your stomach do these gargling high jumps. She totally sympathized with the tragedy of getting 19/100 in Sanskrit. And she knew adults can't be trusted. They would make wild promises to make you obey and then refuse to cough up the promised gifts. She just *knew*.

Her characters were all so real. We all have grandmothers like Didima, who know all about making the perfect prawn malai curry and what to do when you have an ear ache. And who never lose their cool when you play in the rain and leave muddy footprints on the living-room floor. Mothers are guaranteed to scream, but the grandma types just order the maid to swab them away and make you drink hot chocolate.

Then she even gets the animals right. Like when Goopy sees these red glowing eyes in the dark and meets a totally evil cow. Everyone says cows are benign creatures, but are they really? Not when you are the height of their udders, they aren't. They have these huge, square, white teeth always chewing away and a tail that flicks across your face. Lila Majumdar knew that the truly child-friendly animals are dogs and cats.

She once wrote that her favourite themes were treasure hunts, ghosts, dacoits and mysteries. So in these stories you'll get funny happenings and weird people, sinister men with handkerchiefs tied around their noses and a double dose of pearl necklaces. Also rubies the size of pigeons' eggs and a grandpa in a checked dressing gown talking in the middle of the night with a suspicious thin man with a fat wife. Things happen.

She makes you laugh sure, but her world is also full of strange, sinister and at times pretty unpleasant people. That bearded old man with a benign smile could be planning something dangerous, and can you really trust that bad-tempered woman because she cooks so well? Then there are these dangerous creatures called *hulia* and *hoondar*. I have a confession to make, I didn't really know who or what they were but I was quite sure they were after me.

I think Lila Majumdar never really grew up. Lucky you, reading her stories for the first time.

November 2010   Subhadra Sen Gupta

The Burmese Box

I grabbed Panchu Mama's reed-thin arms and dragged him on board the train. For a good ten minutes or so he squatted on the floor, waving his arms in the air like windmills and squalling at the top of his voice 'Ooohhh, ouch! Help, help! *Mumm—mmy!*' and the like. Then, having exhausted the resources of his lungs, he scrambled on to the seat, fished out an enormous scarlet bandana, wiped his forehead, then examined himself minutely to see whether he was mortally wounded and needed to be treated with arnica and iodine.

Finally, having satisfied himself that he was unscathed, he blew his nose and lifted his skinny legs so that he could rest his tiny feet on the opposite seat. Then he turned to me and said in his reedy little voice, 'You know, when I was very small, I took a swig out of a bottle of Badshahi Laxative, double strength! By mistake, of course. My constitution has never been the same since ... but in my heart of hearts,

I am a lion. Otherwise, would I have the courage to search for Podi-pishi's Burmese box?'

He raised his brows, squinted his eyes and gave me a triumphant look. I stared at him, astonished!

The skinny gentleman in the corner, who along with several small children, a fat wife and a mountain of luggage had been following our conversation with breathless interest, also stared in astonishment.

Panchu Mama ignored all of us and continued, 'I'm going to find that box, the box that's been missing for a hundred years. Me, myself! Do you know, there are precious gems in it, worth a king's ransom? Emeralds the size of a rooster's egg, rubies as big as pigeons' eggs, pearls the size of a duck's egg! There are fistfuls of diamonds in that box, heaps of gold sovereigns. Thousands of folks have waded through rivers of blood for that box, sin has piled on heinous sin to form a Himalayan Range of Sin!—And I ... I am going to be the one to make amends, atone for everyone's crimes and rescue that box!'

I couldn't resist saying, 'Huh! You're petrified of my tame white mice, your legs turn to jelly whenever you see a cow a mile away... what can *you* do?'

'I have the spirit of a lion!' declaimed Panchu Mama grandly. Then he fell absolutely silent.

To soothe his hurt feelings, I brought him a paan, a bottle of sticky lemonade, several samosas, some poori and aloo-dum, rasgulla and *khaja* (a crispy sweet, round and fluffy),

2

all served on a sal leaf plate. Then, when he had been fed and pacified, I asked, 'Where is Podi-pishi's Burmese box, Panchu Mama?'

Panchu Mama sidled closer to me, so close that his bony elbow dug into my waist. At the same time, every hair in his eyebrows stood on end till they looked exactly like a pair of furry caterpillars, and as he lowered his little head towards me, I could feel those caterpillars tickling my forehead.

Panchu Mama lowered his voice to a hoarse murmur and began to tell me the story that had become a part of family history. As I listened, I became aware that the skinny gentleman had left his seat and was now sitting on the other side, as close to Panchu Mama as he could get without actually sitting on his lap! His eyes had become round 'O's of surprise and a small lump in his throat wriggled up and down.

The sight of it, and Panchu Mama's hair-raising tale, sent shivers down my spine!

Panchu Mama said, 'Look here, you're going to your mother's ancestral home for the first time since you developed some brains. You'll have to know something of the family history, you know. Grandfather's aunt, Podi-pishi . . . her name will be written in letters of blood and fire on the pages of History! And yet, what was she? A short, stout widow, clad in white, wearing a *rudraksha* necklace . . . and sneaky enough to slice bread with a corkscrew! She had a lion's spirit, and if you look at it, in a way, I am one of her descendants! She was a superb cook, though. Once she served the Viceroy a curry made of grass . . . and he was astounded. He was reported to have said that with food like this, no wonder our country was in this state today!

'Anyway, our Podi-pishi was on her way to Nimai-khuro's house one freezing cold full-moon night in the month of Magh, sitting in state under the awning of a bullock cart and wrapped comfortably in a thick quilt to ward off the bitter January cold. As the cart trundled through the great thirty-two-acre sal forest, Podi-pishi chewed on her paan and thought of Nimai-khuro.

'Very fishy, that Nimai-khuro, she thought. Living in a huge mansion in the middle of the forest, miles from anywhere, with a horde of followers and sycophants. What was more, he always dressed like a guru-ji, with sandalwood paste smeared on his forehead and the name of the lord ever on his lips! He never did a stroke of work, yet always seemed to have a lot of money to spend and to spare. And he was generous, too; made a lot of donations to charity and so forth. But Nimai-khuro was always very cagey about the source of his wealth. Ask him a leading question, and he would say piously that it was all due to the grace of god. The question was, thought Podi-pishi, why, of all the people in the world, would god choose Nimai-khuro as the recipient of his grace?

'All these thoughts were going through her head when suddenly the still of the night was shattered by a dreadful uproar. A horde of lungi-clad, red-eyed, villainous looking men wearing red turbans, all with weapons of some form or other, descended on Podi-pishi's party with wild yells and hoots. Within seconds they had surrounded the bullock cart, dragged the driver from his seat, removed the bullocks from their traces, and then dragged Romakanto (Podi-pishi's quite useless escort) from the cart and snatched away his snuffbox and the seven-and-a-half annas he had in his purse.

'Finally Podi-pishi descended from the cart and stood in the middle of the road, arms akimbo and eyes blazing. Such was the presence of this short, stout, white-clad lady, with the rudraksha necklace around her neck and her pallu wrapped about her waist, that not a single person dared advance towards her.

'"Hoy, you brigands," she said in stentorian tones. "You've managed to put both my driver and poor old Romakanto out of commission, and I don't know if you've left anything of the bullocks, either. Now you carry me all the way to Nimai-khuro's house, or I don't see *how* I am to reach there on time!"

'The robbers nearly fainted on the spot. "We're that sorry, ma'am, for all the trouble. We di'n't mean any harm, we really di'n't! We'll put everything back, right 'n' proper. But if Nimai-sardar ever hears as how we've gone an' 'ttacked his own kith an' kin, he'll eat us alive, he will. Boo-hoo-hoo!"

'Then they put the bullocks back in harness, patted Romakanto on the head, returned his money, bribed the driver with four annas and themselves guided Podi-pishi and her party to Nimai-khuro's house.

'Podi-pishi was full of glee at having finally solved the secret of Nimai-khuro's wealth!'

Panchu Mama took a deep breath, rolled his eyes and continued, 'It didn't take needle-witted Podi-pishi long to understand that Nimai-khuro was the chief of the dacoits, that this was the source of his vast wealth, and during the rest of the journey she laid her devious plans!

'The party reached Nimai-khuro's house long after midnight. Podi-pishi descended from the bullock cart and faced Nimai-khuro, who had come out to greet his redoubtable relative.

'The redoubtable relative looked him straight in the eye and said, through clenched teeth, "I was attacked by a band of brigands during my journey through the forest. I had to descend from the cart in unseemly haste, thereby ripping a corner of my favourite silk shawl. In addition, I stubbed my right big toe, besides receiving quite a jolt in my opinion about certain people." Podi-pishi glared at Nimai-khuro and continued in the same ominous strain, "I haven't decided *yet* on what to do to bring the culprits to book. Just now, I'll cook my own dinner, *if* you please. Then I'll relax with some paan and decide on my next course of action."

'Khuro went pale, and the nozzle of his favourite silver hookah slipped from his hand. As Podi-pishi brushed past him, he stood aside, standing a little aslant on his huge Vidyasagari slippers, wiggling his moustache wordlessly.

'Podi-pishi looked very pleased with herself. "A whole flock of sinister suspicions are fluttering round in my mind," she said pleasantly. "If you don't want them to fly out into the light of day . . . well, you'd better do something about it, dear boy, and do it quickly!"

'With that, she strolled into the inner quarters of the house, washed her feet with some of the cool drinking water stored in an earthen pot then headed for the kitchen. Here she thrust the meek and mild Khuri, Khuro's wife, out of the way and settled down to cook some pulao for herself, with lashings of ghee and sultanas.

'Khuro followed her slowly to the kitchen and stood by the door, still waving his moustache. "I'll give you fifty rupees if you keep quiet about the dacoits," he said, after a while.

'Podi-pishi ignored him and went on with her cooking.

'Khuro said, "I'll raise that to a hundred." Podi-pishi smiled to herself. "What about . . . five hundred, then?" Podi-pishi coughed, an ominous sound. "A thousand?" Khuro sounded desperate. "Five thousand. I'll . . . I'll open my private strongbox and let you take whatever you want."

'Podi-pishi promptly dropped the ladle she had been holding and strode out of the kitchen. She made her way to Khuro's study and stopped in front of the strongbox. "Key, please," was all she said.

'Khuro hastened to unlock the great iron safe. As he opened the heavy door, the jewels and piles of precious gems flashed and glittered in the light of the rising sun. Khuro must have hoped that Podi-pishi, being a mere female, would be dazzled by the richness before her, would lose her head and be quite unable to decide what to take.

'He had misjudged the "mere female"!

'Podi-pishi leant forward and peered into the safe with an exclamation of delight. "My my! This is Aladdin's Cave of Wonders! . . . You rogue, you brigand, you! You've managed to save a pretty penny, haven't you?" Then she gathered up an armful of jewels and gems, and gold ornaments and coins and put them on the floor.

'There was a red Burmese box inside the safe, with gold dragons painted on the lid and along its side. Podi-pishi pulled it out too, but the minute she tried to open it, Khuro protested loudly. "Hey, leave that alone! It has all my important papers and things in it!"

'Podi-pishi squatted down comfortably on the floor and said, without even looking at Khuro, "Shut up, idiot! Otherwise all your nefarious dealings will be front-page news tomorrow." Khuro said no more. Podi-pishi emptied the box, tossed the papers aside carelessly and filled the box to the brim with the jewels and ornaments. Then she shut and locked it and carried it back to the kitchen, to finish her cooking.

'Podi-pishi remained alert and wakeful for the rest of her stay at Nimai-khuro's. Early the next morning she called for the cart and set off for home, the Burmese box clutched safely under her arm.'

Panchu Mama stopped to draw a long, long breath. I

thrust my head forward, peering into his face, and exclaimed, 'And then? What happened after that?'

The skinny gentleman gasped, 'Yes, what then? What next?'

Panchu Mama glared at him. 'I don't see what concern it is of yours, sir,' he snapped, irritated.

The skinny gentleman looked embarrassed. 'No no,' he stammered. 'It's just that . . . er . . . ahem . . . it's such an exciting tale, that . . .'

Panchu Mama turned away and was just about to resume his story, when I noticed something and hissed in French, 'Hsst! Le eyes, zey are gleetering!'

Panchu Mama ignored my warning, and the avid and totally uncalled-for interest of the skinny man, and went on with his story. 'Podi-pishi travelled back home, through the same sal forest, with only a brief stopover for a picnic lunch of khichri and fries. Then on again, until they finally reached the house at about ten o'clock at night.

'Since no one had expected Pishi to return home so quickly, everyone was startled. The entire family rushed out to help her down from the cart and to hear the exciting tale of the journey through the sal forest and the attack by the dacoits. Of course, no one suspected a possible link between Nimai-khuro and the dacoits . . . and Podi-pishi remained mum on the subject.

'Suddenly the old lady remembered the reason for her hasty return . . . the precious Burmese box! It was still there, tucked under her arm—at least, that's what she thought.

'When she pulled it out, the box had vanished! What

she had carried so carefully all this while was her big paan-box!'

Panchu Mama's hair stood on end and eyes became wide as he continued with the tale of Podi-pishi's Burmese box, and the skinny gentleman and I continued listening with bated breath.

'The Burmese box vanished as though it had never been! Of course, Podi-pishi created a furore that had to be seen to be believed. Such was the hullabaloo she created in the middle of the night that the entire family emerged from their respective rooms and quarters, carrying lanterns, candles, torches and any other means of illumination, and searched the house from top to bottom, to the great detriment of each other's toes!

'As for Podi-pishi, she stood in the middle of the courtyard and yelled steadily. "I tell you, I had the box under my arm the whole way . . . and now you say it's not there! A foot long wooden box can't vanish into thin air just like camphor!" She fumed and fretted, while the entire household searched upstairs and downstairs and in every nook and cranny they could think of.

'Finally she had the bullocks unharnessed from the cart, dismantled the entire cart itself so that every millimetre could be searched, and even went so far as to strip the bullock cart driver and poor Romakanto, so they could be properly searched as well. Finally, when she tried to search underneath the bullocks' tails, those highly sagacious animals, tried beyond endurance, brandished their finely shaped horns that found their mark on Podi-pishi's knees.

'This was the last straw! With a screech that had to be heard to be believed, Podi-pishi sank down on the floor. However, though down, Pishi was certainly not out. She continued her powerful imitation of a drill-sergeant and kept the entire household on its toes for the rest of that night.

'The box, however, had vanished as if it had never existed!

'All this while, everyone had been searching under Podi-pishi's orders without having the faintest clue as to what the box contained. But as the dismal dawn broke over the house, Pishi broke down and revealed the true contents of the Burmese box.

'Wiping her streaming eyes, she wailed, "Oh dear, dear dear! Nimai-khuro had been so happy to see me after all these years that he had filled that box to the brim with precious gems and jewellery. And to think you lot have misplaced such a treasure chest!" That was enough to fire the exhausted family into action once more!

'Well, from all accounts, the search continued for three days and three nights. Nobody got a wink of sleep, no one broke off for a proper meal. Even the garden was dug up from end to end. Everyone eyed everyone else with blackest suspicion, even those who loved each other dearly.'

Panchu Mama paused and the skinny gentleman and I chorused, 'Then? What happened then?'

'Nothing really,' said Panchu Mama, shaking his head. 'For a whole week the entire household remained topsy-turvy. Everyone searched and searched; they forgot to eat and sleep, they went up the stairs and down into the cellars, they poked and ferreted about in every nook and cranny, but to no avail! Mountains of dust and yards of spiders' webs were disturbed, hundreds of ancient broken bottles were discovered, along with innumerable snuffboxes and cigarette cases. Thousands of yellowing pieces of paper were dragged out, many of them highly confidential notes and letters. So many secrets tumbled out into the open, so many lost things were found . . . except for Podi-pishi's Burmese box. It had vanished into thin air!

'In fact, many people were heard muttering darkly amongst themselves that the box was just a figment of Pishis's over-active imagination, that there never had been a box of any sort. Only poor old Romakanto kept insisting that there *had* been some sort of a box, Podi-pishi had it with her when she had left Nimai-khuro's house. He had not seen it with his own eyes, said Romakanto, as it had been covered with Podi-pishi's voluminous shawl. But he had not only made out its large, square shape, he had also been poked in the tummy with one of its sharp corners. And it had not been Pishi's ample paan-box, because Romakanto had felt its sharp corner prodding his spine.

'The loss of the Burmese box affected even the normally resilient Podi-pishi very badly. So many gems and golden guineas and pieces of jewellery, people could spend a lifetime without seeing even a fraction of that amount; and she had had it in her hand and it had vanished into thin air! The thought of it sent Pishi into a decline. When she managed to pull herself together, she took Romakanto and went to meet Nimai-khuro, probably hoping to recoup her loss. But the thirty-two-acre sal forest seemed oddly empty and quiet, and when she finally reached the mansion that had been Nimai-khuro's headquarters, she found the house deserted and in ruins, home only to wild cats and owls.

'Well, that was that! Years passed and most of the family forgot about the box and the brouhaha it had caused; some remembered it vaguely, like an ancient family legend. Only Podi-pishi used to bemoan the loss once in a while, but that became rarer as she grew older and frailer. Just before she passed away, however, she managed to give the family one last shock! She was practically bedridden at that time, when she suddenly chuckled to herself and said, "Oh my goodness me! *Now* I remember what I did with the box!" And she shut her eyes and slipped away calmly.

'It was enough to send the family into a tizzy! Everyone waited until the *shraddh* ceremony was over; then they went through the house once more with a fine-tooth comb. But no one found any trace of the Burmese box.'

The skinny gentleman gasped, 'Then?'

Panchu Mama said grandiosely, 'I will find that box!' Then he snapped irritably, 'But what is it to you, sir?'

He glared so ferociously that the skinny gentleman scuttled on to his own bench and sat down, picking his teeth and studiously ignoring us. By then it was quite late and his fat wife and the three children had gone to sleep, in a huge heap on the bunk.

I sat waiting for Panchu Mama to reveal some more interesting and hair-raising family secrets, but he merely kicked off his slippers and prepared to go to sleep. This was most frustrating, as there were umpteen things I wanted to know. It seemed that the skinny gentleman felt the same, for he stopped picking his teeth and said, 'If that box has been missing for a hundred years or more, what makes you think that you can find it? Have you uncovered some new fact, or found a footprint or fingerprint, or some such thing?'

I must admit that he had a point!

Panchu Mama answered solemnly, 'Well, I haven't found anything *yet*, but it's only a matter of time. After all, Podipishi's last words were significant. I am inclined to think that the box is there somewhere, right under our noses. We'll only have to use our eyes to find it. After all, she barely had any time after her return from Nimai-khuro's to hide such a box. So it must be right there somewhere! And her chuckle when she did finally remember must mean that it had not been stolen. But if I've said it once, I've said it a hundred times, what concern is it to you, my dear sir?'

The skinny gentleman did not answer; instead, he pulled a sheet over his head and settled down to sleep.

Gradually everyone followed his example, stretched out on their bunks. But I sat by the window, wide awake, and watched the dance of a thousand fireflies in the dark bushes lining the tracks, and the occasional fleck of a burning ember in the plume of smoke billowing from the engine. Slowly, all these became dim and dark and far away; instead, floating in front of my eyes was an enormous red Burmese box, and painted on its side was a great black dragon spouting fire and flames from its eyes and nose, its forked tongue sticking out. Then the lid of the box opened and I saw it was filled with a dazzling array of gems . . . enormous gems, rubies, emeralds, pearls . . .

With a screech and grinding of brakes the train came to a stop.

It was nearly midnight when we reached our destination. A cold wind blew through the branches of the spruce trees lining the fence behind the station. Panchu Mama and I descended and looked around the deserted platform. The only living creature was the stationmaster standing by the tiny station building, swinging a smoky lantern. He hadn't shaved in days, I noticed, and he was yawning widely, showing his paan-stained teeth. Otherwise there was nothing—no car or horse, no bullock cart, not even a cat!

I looked at Panchu Mama; he looked back with a pale, frightened face. I snapped in annoyance, 'You always say we're the zamindars of this area, and everyone here is our loyal subject. Is this an example of that? I'd thought that there'd be torches blazing and a band would be playing for us, and a red carpet rolled out for our welcome. People would throng around with garlands and bouquets, and we'd drive home in a coach-and-four! And when we reached there, there'd be a hot ...'

At this point Panchu Mama edged closer to me and hissed in my ear, 'Shut up, idiot! Can't you see, we're surrounded by danger as dark as this night? Bloodthirsty vampires are at our heels, is this the time to fight amongst ourselves?'

I jumped and stopped midway through my harangue. Looking around, I saw that the skinny gentleman, a dim torch in his hand, was pulling his wife, children and several enormous bundles off the train. As soon as they had stepped out, the train moved off with a loud rumble and hiss; a deathly silence fell over the station, broken only by Panchu Mama's heavy breathing close to my ears. Then the silence was shattered by a stentorian voice bawling, 'Hoy Panchu Dada! Hey there, Mejdimoni's little lad! 'Ave ye come, or 'aven't ye, then?'

I jumped nearly out of my skin, but Panchu Mama reacted as though he had seen a Vision. He raced forward, exclaiming, 'Ghanshyam! You've come at last! Oh, thank goodness!'

Far from being pleased, however, Ghanshyam exclaimed in annoyance, 'Well! Ye took yer time, di'n't ye? Now, stop yer blatherin', Panchu Dada, an' tell me wot I'm to do. Th' big bullock as I brought along-a me, 'e's a-sittin' there, as comfy as ye please, chewin' of th' cud, an' nothin' as I said or did, no, not even me a-twistin' of 'is tail or tryin' to get 'im off th' ground wi' a bamboo ... nothin' would make 'im budge!'

Panchu Mama looked alarmed. 'Oh dear! Ghanshyam, what are we to do, then?'

'Do? I dunno wot t' do, meself,' Ghanshyam said in disgruntled tones. 'Come away an' take a look.'

We followed Ghanshyam through a gate in the fence to the dusty road behind the station. There, standing at an angle on side, was a cart; one bullock was still attached to it, looking hopelessly at its mate snoozing comfortably on the road a little distance away.

Try as we might, that bullock just refused to get up from its comfortable position. Finally Ghanshyam gave up in disgust, piled our luggage and us on the cart and strapped himself into the traces beside the other bullock. He gave an almighty pull and, to our great surprise, the cart began to move forward quite easily.

Just past the station and a little to the right was an ancient graveyard. Enormous willows stood here and there, their branches waving in the breeze, adding to the spooky darkness of the place. Panchu Mama said softly, 'Most of the graves here go back to the time of the Mutiny.'

Immediately Ghanshyam stopped and turned to glare at Panchu Mama. 'Don't ye dare go a-tellin' the lad stories o' spooks an' sich-like, Panchu Dada,' he snapped. 'Ye do that, an' I'll jes' drop me 'arness an' leg it fer 'ome, so 'elp me, I will.'

'Oh no no, Ghanshyam,' Panchu Mama said anxiously. 'I wasn't telling him ghost stories, just about the graves.'

'Well, an' wot's th' difference one t'other?' demanded Ghanshyam, hands on his hips. 'Grave to ye, spook to *me*, I says. Jes' coz ye c'n tell of it in English, ye thinks as I cu'n't unnerstand eh? Well, I know yer tricksy ways, that I do, an' it won't work nohow, Panchu Dada, an' so I tell ye.' With that, he really did drop the traces and moved away from the cart.

Just then we heard the rattle of wheels, and a shabby horse-drawn cab whirled past us in a cloud of dust. As it drew level, I saw the skinny gentleman in the shadowy interior; he was staring at us with gleaming eyes.

Instantly Panchu Mama flung out his arms and legs and fell back in a dead faint.

Ghanshyam gave him a disgusted look. 'Stop bein' so silly, Panchu Dada,' he said. Then he picked up the traces and began to move forward again. Panchu Mama heaved an enormous sigh, sat up and wiped his face with a large bandana.

It was well past midnight when we reached my mother's ancestral home. As we approached the huge old mansion, I suddenly remembered that on just such a night as this Podi-pishi had returned home from Nimai-khuro's secret hideout. With her had been Romakanto and the fabled Burmese box. Really, where had that box gone? Suddenly a thought struck me and I turned to my uncle and asked, 'Did it slip out from under her arms? Perhaps that's why . . .'

'Hsshh, quiet!' Panchu Mama hissed through clenched teeth. 'Remember, you are entering the enemy's lair. Don't even hint at the Burmese box, no, not even if they pull your still-beating heart from your body!'

Ghanshyam pulled the cart as far as the front porch; then he collapsed on the steps, wiping his face and fanning himself with his face cloth. As soon as we descended from the cart, a horde of cousins of every shape and size appeared out of thin air. They gathered around us, staring as if we were freaks escaped from the nearest circus, but no one helped us take our luggage off the cart. Even Panchu Mama drifted off somewhere through the crowd. Finally, feeling extremely irritated with everyone, I began to pull the cases and bundles off the cart and fling them on to the floor.

The noise I made brought Didima, my grandmother, to the front door. Seeing me, she hugged and kissed me, right in front of all those folk. Then, having shooed away the crowd, she took me to meet Shejodadamoshai, my mother's uncle.

Shejodadamoshai was an impressive figure with his handlebar moustache, fierce eyes and sleek hair. He sat in an enormous easy chair, covered with a quilt, and glared at me under beetling brows. My heart skipped a beat when I saw him, and I realized that here was Enemy No.1! However, I followed Didima into the room and touched his feet in a respectful pranam. He merely smiled and said, 'Hmmm!'

Suddenly I felt annoyed. Not scared any more but very, very angry. I followed Didima downstairs to the dining room and sat down on the seat used by my grandfather many years ago. Didima served dinner—poori, dal, fried brinjal, cauliflower curry, prawn malai curry, chutney, kheer, rasgullas—and I dug in with relish and without bothering about anyone else. I kept eating and my grandmother kept the good things coming, until I could eat no more. Only then did I notice that Panchu Mama had come into the room and was seated in a corner, picking quietly at his food.

I glanced at him once or twice, but my uncle continued to ignore me, behaving as though I was a complete stranger. It made me feel so unhappy, especially when Panchu Mama turned his face away from me. But when we went to wash our hands after the meal, he hissed in my ear, 'Better not show too much familiarity, my boy, or they'll suspect something at once. The old lady is Spy No.1!'

I protested at this, for I was very fond of Didima. But Panchu Mama glared at me and snapped, 'Don't argue! I know my own aunt better than you do!'

Later, I followed Didima up the great wooden staircase to her bedroom. It was a huge room, but was dwarfed by the bed in the centre. I have never seen such an incredible piece of furniture, covered with amazing carvings and so high that you had to climb up two wooden steps to get in it. There were two or three enormous bolsters on the bed, and under the bed were several brass pots, urns and such-like articles.

Didima set down the candle-stand on a brightly painted stool, tucked me in, patted my head and said, 'Go to sleep, darling, you must be very tired after your journey. I'll just go downstairs and finish my dinner, then I'll come up and sleep here beside you. Tomorrow night I'll tell you the story of Podi-pishi and her Burmese box.' At the mention of Podi-pishi's name, my heart began to beat very fast. Didima continued, 'You won't feel scared lying here all alone for a while, will you, dear?'

I said, 'Leave the candle here, and I won't feel scared.'

Didima gave me a kiss and went downstairs. She is such a dear, I thought. Why did Panchu Mama call her Spy No.1?

I don't know when I fell asleep or when Didima came up to sleep beside me. I woke up very early in the morning, but Didima had already gone downstairs. So I got up as well, scrambled off the bed and went out to the balcony outside the room. The garden and the mango orchards beyond were covered with swirling rags of mist, blown hither and thither by the chill morning breeze. It may have been because of this, or because of what I saw just at the edge of the orchard, that I felt a cold shiver run up my spine.

Standing under a mango tree was our skinny acquaintance of the train. He was wearing a grey woollen suit and a muffler wrapped about his head and neck, and he was scrutinizing the house with a pair of powerful binoculars.

My tonsils nearly jumped out of my throat at the sight!

Just then the skinny gentleman turned and vanished into the shadows under the ancient mango trees, and the first rays of the early morning sun broke through the mists and filled the garden with a golden glow. There was the sound of heavy footsteps and I turned to see Shejodadamoshai, wearing a red-and-blue checked lungi and a green woollen dressing gown, standing beside me. He was chewing on a mango twig . . . to sharpen his teeth, perhaps.

Shejodadamoshai said, 'D'you know, this room and this balcony was the domain of my uncle . . . my Chhoto-kaka. He had gone to England for higher studies, and when he returned, he was a true English gentleman! Hair cut very short, wouldn't wear anything but suits from Bond Street, a cane in hand and a cigar between his lips, speaking in clipped King's English, liberally interspersed with swear words!

'We had barely recovered from the shock of his changed appearance when he announced that he had decided to marry an Englishwoman and bring her home. He would renovate the big bedroom and the veranda and build an attached bathroom; what was more, there would be a spiral staircase leading up from the garden, and a sweeper in a white turban would come up that to clean the rooms.

'You can imagine the pandemonium amongst the female members of the family!

'"A *mem*!" they wailed in chorus. "Oh goodness! They have red hair and light eyes, their complexion as pale as death warmed up, and stick-like figures! *And* they eat all sorts of unmentionables, too, we've heard!"

'Chhoto-kaka was annoyed. "Well, if you want me to become a sannyasi and renounce the world, just say the word," he snapped. "I'll become a Naga sannyasi, covered in ashes and wearing no clothes, if you like. Then I won't need either my English wife or my new suits!"

'That brought on another chorus of wails. But everyone was so scared of my grandfather that they didn't dare breathe a word of all this to him!'

Shejodadamoshai continued, still chewing on his stick, 'Chhoto-kaka didn't waste any time. He organized an army of workmen and had that spiral staircase installed in short order. See that corner? That's where the railing was cut away for the head of the spiral staircase. There was a wooden staircase going up to the terrace from the second floor, for chasing away monkeys. The new staircase was fixed just below that. Once that was done, only the construction of the new bathroom and buying the sweeper's uniform remained. Chhoto-kaka began to lay plans on how to wangle the extra cash out of Grandfather.

'In the meantime, the new staircase turned out to be a boon and blessing for the local thieves' community. They started frequenting our house every night, running happily up and down the spiral stairs. It became impossible to go to sleep, thanks to the racket they made!

'And one night their merrymaking woke Grandfather. He picked up his huge club and stalked out to the veranda. The thieves took one look at his redoubtable figure, fled down the stairs and vanished into the darkness. Grandfather stared in astonishment at the brand new staircase glinting in the moonlight. Then, without saying a word or asking any questions, he went quietly back to his room and to sleep.'

Shejodadamoshai drew a deep breath and went on. 'The next morning he sent for his own set of workmen and had the spiral staircase dismantled without further ado. What's more, he also told them to get rid of the wooden monkey-chasing stairs and repair the cut off railings.

'Then he summoned Chhoto-kaka and said, "I've arranged your marriage with my friend Panu's younger daughter. Go and get ready." And within a few days Chhoto-kaka was married to that fair, fat, round-eyed twelve-year-old daughter of his father's friend, and they lived happily ever after. They really did! Our Panchu is their grandson! . . . Oh goodness, here comes Ghanshyam with my daily dose of Isabgol! Tell him I've gone out!'

And Shejodadamoshai vanished like the morning mist.

I turned to look, and saw that the niches where the wooden staircase had been fixed were still there, cut deeply into the wall.

So Shejodadamoshai hadn't been making things up!

Like all old houses, my mother's ancestral house had enormous rooms with high ceilings, broad staircases and verandas so long that if someone called from one end, it was inaudible at the other. And in the afternoon, it became as silent as a graveyard.

I hadn't seen hair or hide of Panchu Mama since early morning. If we hadn't travelled down in the same train, I wouldn't have known he even existed. There wasn't any proof that he had been born on this planet! Nobody in the house so much as breathed his name. Amazing!

After lunch, I was rooting about the house, looking for the infamous Burmese box, when I heard the sounds of great merry-making coming from the direction of the kitchen, as though some festivity was going on there.

What was afoot?

I crept forward and peered cautiously round the bend in the passage leading to the kitchen quarters. And what I saw made me nearly swallow my tongue in astonishment.

All the servants were out there in full force, entertaining a guest . . . a skinny, long-legged person who had the place of honour on our cook's own stool; he seemed thoroughly at ease, sitting with his legs stretched out before him. Piles of paan and cheap cigarettes lay scattered about. Even our cook was smoking like a chimney under her saree pallu!

The moment they heard my footsteps, the veranda emptied in an instant, as though someone had waved a magic wand. One moment the servants were all there, the next they weren't! Only the cook remained, yawning elaborately behind her saree; she'd even managed to hide away her half-smoked cigarette.

But I had seen enough. That long-legged guest was none other than our skinny fellow traveller!

What bravado, I thought! What guts! He had checked out the lay of the land with his binoculars that very morning, and by lunchtime was right inside! My hair stood on end until my head looked like the back of a healthy hedgehog.

I turned to the cook and asked, 'Who was that skinny fellow?'

She pretended to be astonished. 'Which fellow, my child?' she asked. 'There's no one here but you and me.' As she moved away, I heard the chink of silver coins in her lap.

So he had bribed the servant community! Goodness, how deviously evil!

I needed to discuss the matter with Panchu Mama, but where on earth was he? He seemed to have gone undercover since early morning. I had heard a rumour about halfway through the morning that he had taken a large dose of laxative by mistake and had retired from public view thereafter. Still, I had to locate him, so I set off in search of my uncle.

After opening three or four wrong doors, and being yelled at three or four times by several irate relatives, I finally ran my missing uncle to earth in a small room in the East Wing. He was lying curled up on a divan, rubbing his tummy with a morose expression on his face. The moment he set eyes on me, he scowled and exclaimed in wheezy tones, 'Why have you come here, you pest? Go away!'

I said solemnly, 'Is this the time to snuggle down comfortably in bed and rub your tummy? We are surrounded by evil plots and counterplots; the enemy has stormed the citadel!'

Instead of bounding out of bed and helping me, Panchu Mama let forth such a chorus of whines that I was forced to retire from his room with what dignity I could muster.

The rest of that day I spent in trying to figure out what my next course of action should be in trying to locate that fabulous box, but I couldn't think of a single sensible thing to do.

That night, as I snuggled down under my quilt, Didima finished her work and came to lie down beside me. 'I'll tell you the story of Podi-pishi and her Burmese box, just as I promised,' she said, stroking my head.

Didima wrapped herself in her own green quilt, stuffed a paan inside her mouth and settled back comfortably, while I listened with bated breath to this colourful chapter in our family's history.

'Do you know, our Podi-pishi was built like an all-in wrestler—bulging chest muscles, massive biceps and triceps! Every morning she would down a litre of milk with about half a kilo of sprouted grams. And what a ferocious personality! I've heard stories of how, when a large black cow disturbed her afternoon siesta with its constant bellows, she stalked out and gave it such a glare that for the next three days the cow gave yoghurt instead of milk.

'One chilly winter morning, Podi-pishi and her faithful servant Romakanto set off in a bullock cart for goodness only knows where. She didn't bother to inform anyone about where she was going, or why, or even when she expected to be back. Didn't think it necessary, I suppose!

'She returned at midnight . . . and instantly started such a hullabaloo as has to be seen and heard to be believed! Apparently she had mislaid a Burmese box. Do you know, dear, we searched for that wretched box for a year and a half, although none of us had set eyes on it. And it never was found!'

I asked breathlessly, 'What was in the box?'

'I have no idea,' said Didima. 'Most probably paan-masala or something like that. Now, Podi-pishi had only one weakness . . . her only son Goja, a skinny, dark youth with a head of oily curls cut in the latest style. Always dressed in the height of fashion, too, in the finest muslin kurtas and pink vests. He spent the whole day idling, smoking or chewing paan; he never did a stroke of work, didn't even study in school, let alone do a sensible job of work. Only tootled round with his equally useless friends. His only activity was gossip or taking part in local plays. Yet no one dared say a word for fear of Podi-pishi's wrath!'

Didima sighed lugubriously. 'The good people of this world never have any good fortune . . . that's the law of Nature! The most successful are the crooks, cheats and rascals. That Goja was a perfect example of this immutable law! As he grew older, and his horns and tails became more pronounced, he learnt all the tricks of the trade—opium addiction, card-sharping and the like. Occasionally he would vanish for a couple of months. Then he would turn up unexpectedly, grinning from ear to ear and showing paan-stained teeth, and Podi-pishi would move heaven and earth to provide her precious darling with all the money he wanted.

'Goja was on cloud nine!

'Then, suddenly, there was an incredible change in Goja. He began to treat his dumbfounded family with barrels of meat curry and mountains of the best sweets. During winter, he brought woollen vests for all the servants. He brought a horse-and-carriage, he started sporting a diamond ring. The entire family had a collective heart attack! Where on earth did Goja get so much money? Even Podi-pishi was worried.

'Having a lot of money was very good, but where did it come from?'

I fell asleep listening to the story of Master Goja. I woke up suddenly in the middle of the night. It was so still and quiet, I could hear all sorts of weird and unlikely sounds—faint snores from my grandmother, invisible behind the mountain of bolsters; the distant hoot of a barn owl; creaks and crackles as the great teak beams overhead settled down for the night.

All these strange sounds . . . but they hadn't woken me. It was something far more mysterious . . . skin-crawling, hair-raisingly mysterious! I lay there, stiff as a board, too scared to move a muscle. But for how long? Finally, when I just couldn't lie there any more, when my legs itched to move, and my throat became so dry that I had to have a gulp of water, I crept out from under the protection of my quilt and clambered down the steps.

Very, very slowly I opened the door and came outside. Three large jugs of water stood on a low table a little further down the passage. But how to reach them? I had to cross the black darkness separating me and them . . . and I didn't want to!

I stood there, scratching my left calf with my right big toe, when I heard a sound!

I almost fainted in fright.

The sound came from the direction of Shejodadamoshai's room. In my mind's eye I clearly saw a horde of skinny, well-oiled brigands in red loincloths and gold earrings, a dagger held between their teeth, cutting holes in the brick wall of Shejodadamoshai's room with their special tools. And after entering in their hundreds, rummaging through Shejodadamoshai's cash box, purloining his silver hookah, walking away in his velvet bedroom slippers.

Just then Shejodadamoshai's bedroom door swung open with a faint squeak, and someone came out, lighting an evil-smelling *beedi*. In the brief flare of the match I recognized the night-time prowler at once—none other than our skinny fellow traveller! He was creeping out of the room, his shoes tucked safely under his arm.

I stood paralysed, prepared for death by violence. But the fellow stubbed his toe on a nail or something, muttered 'Dash it!' and vanished into the darkness. A few minutes later I heard a door shut somewhere.

By then, my arms and legs had returned to their normal state of living. I decided against a drink of water, life-saving or no. After all, I had just escaped from the clutches of a skinny fellow, but the next one might be a hulking bandit . . . and I might not be so lucky!

I turned to get back to the safety of my bedroom, when a piece of paper came fluttering out of nowhere and wrapped itself around my leg. I picked it up and had just pushed it into my pocket when Shejodadamoshai's bedroom door opened again and my grand-uncle came shuffling out with a torch in his hand, looking harassed, and began hunting all around for something . . . no doubt that piece of paper. I stood in the darkness, as still as a mouse, frightened nearly out of my wits! If I was spotted . . .

I was lucky again, for Shejodadamoshai stubbed his toe on the same nail, muttered a hundred-and-one unprintable stuff under his breath, then limped back into his room, probably to treat his injured limbs.

I drew a long breath, drank some water and slipped back into my room, not quite sure as to what I should do. The piece of paper rustled and crackled in my pocket, but Didima had switched off the lights so reading it just then was impossible. Of course, there was a candle and matchbox on the brightly coloured stool in the corner. But I didn't want everyone to know everything just yet, so I resisted the temptation and waited for the morning

I must have fallen asleep while waiting. And I dreamed that Podi-pishi came in through the veranda door and called to me. A strong, muscular lady she was, just as family lore presented her, dressed in white with a rudraksha necklace about her neck, hair cropped short and a sandalwood paste dot on her forehead.

She matched Panchu Mama's description to a T.

One hand was hidden behind her back and she beckoned me with the other. I followed her out to the veranda and as soon as I reached her side, she asked, 'Found the box, boy?' I shook my head and said, 'No, not yet. Where did you hide the box all in a moment? People have been hunting for it all these years and they still haven't found it. What can *I* do in two days?' She said, 'Look properly. When you find it, you can have it. That Panchu is an idiot, can't even take a proper dose of laxative, and he wants to be the world's best detective! Huh! No, *you* have the box. There's a pair of ruby earrings in it; give it to your mother. Oh, and one more thing, find the box and make that old fellow and his skinny sidekick look a pair of fools. And don't worry about my precious Goja. Thanks to the grace of Baba Bishwanath, he's just fine; he's bought a house, a carriage-and-pair and has started his own opium business.' She sighed and went on, 'Only Baba Bishwanath in all His grace cares for the sinners and criminals. Otherwise, who would even look at them?'

Then she kissed me and turned to stalk down the infamous spiral stairs built for his English lady by Chhoto-kaka. As she turned away, I saw she was carrying an enormous club in the hand she had hidden behind her back!

I gasped in surprise . . . and woke up with a start. It was morning already. Sunlight flooded in through the door leading out to the veranda, spilling warmly over the bed and catching the niches that had held the wooden monkey-chasing ladder.

Suddenly I felt . . . and I don't know why . . . that that ladder was very, very important!

I sat up in bed, feeling excited. Didima had gone down, I was all alone. This was the perfect time to see what was written in that paper. I pulled it out of my pocket, spread it out and read:

Received from Shri Bipin Bihari Choudhury a sum of Rs 200/—(Rupees Two hundred) only.
Signed: Nidhiram Sharma.
N.B.—All investigations to be strictly private and confidential.

I thought, why had Shejodadamoshai paid the skinny one? What investigations? This was highly suspicious!

Suddenly the door flew open, Panchu Mama shot in, shut the door and stood leaning against, gasping like a stranded catfish. His face was an interesting shade of greenish-white, his forehead was beaded with sweat and his hair stood on end.

I tucked the letter back in my pocket, jumped off the bed and asked, 'What's the matter? Have you taken another dose of Milk of Magnesia?'

Panchu Mama licked his dry lips with an even drier tongue and croaked, 'Khenti-pishi has come!'

'Who on earth is Khenti-pishi?'

In a voice of doom, Panchu Mama said, 'Podi-pishi the Second!'

I pulled the letter out of my pocket and waved it under Panchu Mama's nose. 'Don't worry about such trivial matters as the arrival of some female relative!' I said. 'Do you know, Shejodadamoshai himself is involved in this affair? Look, I have proof positive.'

Panchu Mama took the letter and was just going to read it, when the door was pushed open with unbelievable force and . . . believe it or not . . . a carbon copy of Podi-pishi that I had seen in my dream stumped into the room, her expression thunderous.

So *this* was Khenti-pishi, Podi-pishi's niece!

The force with which she had opened the door had sent Panchu Mama flying across the room. He landed on my bed with a thump and began to hurl defiance at Khenti-pishi in a shrill voice. 'What can *you* do to me? D'you know, there isn't a woman born who can frighten me! D'you know, a lion roars . . .' At which point Khenti-pishi wrapped her pallu about her waist and took a step towards Panchu Mama.

The sight of her stealthily advancing form was enough to send my uncle diving for cover. He scuttled under the bed and vanished among the mountain of pots and pans that were stored there.

Robbed of her rightful prey, Khenti-pishi turned her gimlet eyes on me. She swept me from head to foot with such a burning glance that I shrivelled on the spot. The paper in my hand rustled loudly, and Khenti-pishi reacted as though she had been shot!

She moved forward . . . perhaps to pounce on me and tear me to pieces . . . when the door opened again and Shejodadamoshai came in. He scowled when he saw my formidable aunt.

'Oh, it's you, Khenti!' he huffed. 'What do *you* want here?'

Khenti-pishi turned her 1000-watt power eyes on him . . . and I'll say this for Shejodadamoshai, he didn't wilt! She said in icy tones, 'Why, what's your problem? I didn't get a single thing from you last Puja, and the shirt you sent my Bhoja was cheap and ugly, absolute rubbish! I never get a thing from here, my own father's home, no, not even half a banana. But does that mean I won't find a place in my sister-in-law's room?'

Panchu Mama stuck out his head between two large pots and yelled, 'Whether you get a place or not is not your concern! And what's the reason for invading my private quarters at this unearthly hour . . .' Khenti-pishi turned towards him and his head vanished as rapidly as a tortoise's.

Shejodadamoshai cleared his throat and said, 'Panchu, you rascal, come out of there this instant and help me find an important paper I have lost. Come on, out you get. You'd better help me, or it'll be the worse for you!'

Khenti-pishi, too, added her two bits. 'Get out from under the bed, you twit!' she snarled. 'You must've removed the plan of this house from my suitcase. Come on out, I'm going to search you from head to toe. I know what you're after, you little rat! Podi-pishi's Burmese box! Well, let me tell you, only I have a right to that box; it's a part of my dowry!'

Shejodadamoshai said furiously, 'What d'you mean . . . only you have a right to it? All you'll do is hand it over to your precious Bhoja. I'm a trained lawyer, as you *should* know, and only *I* have a right to that box! Besides, I've paid a professional detective two hundred rupees to find that box. And find it I will!'

A soft cough came from the doorway. We turned and saw the skinny gentleman, clad in a long black Ulster, leaning against the doorpost and smoking like a chimney. He removed the evil-smelling beedi from his mouth just long enough to say, 'Remember, a third of whatever's in that box is mine. If you do find that box, it'll be because of my incredible brains.'

Khenti-pishi suddenly discovered Panchu Mama's skinny legs sticking out from under the bed. That was all she needed. She pounced on my unfortunate uncle and dragged him out, kicking and squealing. Khenti-pishi stood him upright, shook him, gave him a ringing slap, then pulled out a folded piece of paper from his front pocket.

'How dare you say you didn't rummage around in my suitcase and take the plan? Oh goodness gracious me! Just look, Shej-da, it's his report card. He's got nineteen in Sanskrit! *Nineteen* per cent!'

Shejodadamoshai clicked his tongue and said, 'Let's have a look!'

And the skinny detective added piously, 'He can hardly be called an educated human being, can he?'

Panchu Mama had suddenly realized he was free. He dived under the bed again. From the safety of his refuge, he yelled shrilly, 'What's it to you how I've fared in my college exams? Especially an illiterate female like Khenti-pishi! Lost your plans, have you? Mislaid your important papers? It's your fault, and all you do is attack a poor, innocent fellow like me. And all the time no one bothers to find out what paper that young imp in knickerbockers has in his hand!'

The traitor! Blackleg! Turncoat!

But I had no time to protest.

Khenti-pishi, Shejodadamoshai, the skinny detective, all forgot their individual arguments, forgot Panchu Mama's shocking Sanskrit marks even, and stalked forward towards me.

They were going to corner me!

I heard their hissing breaths. I had to take evasive action.

I let out a yell of 'Didima, help!' and shot out of the room and on to the veranda. Looking round in a hunted fashion, I suddenly understood why the niches of the monkey-chasing ladder had felt so important. Their work wasn't over yet!

It took me only a minute or two to dig my fingers and toes into those cuts and swarm up the wall to the safety of the upper terrace. Once there, I flopped down and lay sprawled out on the sunny floor, panting like a bellows.

I was safe! Hungry, but safe.

Not one of those downstairs would be able to climb up here.

As the sun rose higher, the whole upper terrace was flooded with warm, honey-gold light. A cool breeze blew through my toes, bringing with it the scent of the trees. The terrace was carpeted with dry leaves, accumulated over the years, and they rustled and whispered softly in the breeze. The only other sound was the cooing of hundreds and hundreds of pigeons fluttering in and out of the niches carved into the sides of the great dome that dominated the front of the terrace. There was a distinct smell of pigeons all around.

I sat up and watched them idly, feeling very hungry, but knowing that I wouldn't be safe anywhere else but here. If I so much as set a toe downstairs, I would be grabbed and . . . no doubt . . . tortured!

I decided to remain up here, where I was safe from my enemies. I would stay there for the whole day, I thought, and for the entire night, if need be!

There wasn't anything to do, except watch the pigeons and listen to them as they cooed and bubbled and gurgled in a hundred different tones and timbres. There were masses of them, roosting on the parapet, flying up into the air and down again into the dome with its carved and fretworked walls.

I got up and went towards the dome. This was the kingdom of the pigeons—there were literally thousands of them, roosting in the carved niches. There were red-faced babies staring at me in astonishment and their agitated mothers yelling rude things at me. Hundreds more fluttering in and out of those niches where they had their nests, every niche a safe haven . . . except two, far above me near the top of the dome.

Those two were empty!

Suddenly I felt cold, even in the warm sunshine. Every

hair on my head stood up as rigid as guardsmen and my legs turned to jelly. I heard a loud thundering in my ear— it was my heart beating unnaturally loudly. Only one thought now kept going through my mind: was I going to be the one to find what everyone in the family had been seeking for the past hundred years? I, who had never got more than forty in maths!

Was I to be the one who rediscovered Podi-pishi's Burmese box?

Suddenly my legs became legs again, and not some carving made of softened butter. I knew what I had to do, so I scrambled up the side of the dome and dropped down inside it.

I noticed that the dome was solid on all sides except at the centre. There was dampness inside and the floor was carpeted with pigeon feathers. And scrawled on the inside wall in somewhat skewed letters were the words *'Goja's Haven and Only Shelter'*.

I looked up towards the empty niches. The rear side was visible from within the dome, and behind the niches was a rough wooden shelf. It took up a portion of the niches, which was why the pigeons hadn't been able to use it for their nests.

Which was what had roused my suspicions!

I reached up and lifted down a medium-sized box that had been tucked away at the back of the shelf. Incredibly, it was still as bright and gleaming as if it was brand new. The green eyes of the dragon painted on the lid glittered as though it was alive.

I put the box on my lap and gingerly raised the lid. On top was a bunch of handmade paper, yellow with age, threaded through with a red cord. On one side of each sheet were some lines written in Sanskrit, on the other, the same skewed letters that were etched on the wall . . . Goja's handwriting!

I removed the papers and looked in eagerly. The box was full of beautiful necklaces, bracelets and earrings, some of gold, some studded with gems of many hues—red and green, blue and yellow and white. There was also a pair of ruby earrings, just as Podi-pishi had said. I slipped them into my pocket; after all, this was Podi-pishi's box and *she* had asked me to give them to my mother.

I picked up the papers and tried to read what Goja had written, but it was beyond me. I would have to give it to Shejodadamoshai; only he would be able to decipher Goja's hieroglyphs! And the box I'd hand over to Didima, so she could distribute the jewels as she thought fit.

And I forgave them all! I forgave them for scaring me, and surrounding me, and chasing after me. I didn't feel a bit angry any more.

I'd rather forget my journey down.

How I scrambled up the inner wall of the dome, clutching the box to my chest, and then scrambled down the outer side without dropping my precious load, I'll never know. As for getting down the broken monkey-chasing ladder— I must have developed superhuman powers, for I'm sure I'll never be able to repeat that feat ever again.

When I finally reached the safety of the veranda, I found my relatives still standing in a bristling circle. But the moment they saw what I carried in my hands—the lost Burmese box—they were paralysed with shock and surprise. All they could do was gape at me in utter disbelief!

I ignored them all, called for Didima and handed the box over to her. The bunch of papers I gave to Shejodadamoshai. He took it in a dazed fashion and absent-mindedly began to turn over the pages. The skinny fellow, as usual, sidled up to my grand-uncle and tried to peer over his shoulder to get a glimpse of the century-old papers. However, as Shejodadamoshai was very tall and the skinny man very short, he didn't meet with very great success.

Suddenly Shejodadamoshai exclaimed, 'Goodness, these are the wedding mantras that disappeared during Podi-pishi's younger sister Moni-pishi's marriage. The priest tried to say the mantras from memory, made several awful mistakes, and the result was that Moni-pishi and her husband spent their entire life arguing with each other!'

Then he turned over the bunch to read the other side, and said in astonished tones, 'Listen to what Podi-pishi's dearest Goja has written! It's like a diary of sorts, although the less said about his handwriting and his spellings the better. And no date, nothing. So Goja was the culprit, snitching the papers during his aunt's wedding ceremony and making a diary of it.'

And Shejodadamoshai read: '*Monday—Great disaster hath befallen me. My respected Mother returned, and upon* reaching the house, descended from the cart and first thrust the Burmese box into mine hands. And she hast then forgotten the act and hath commenced chastising the entire household for no cause, as usual.

'Tuesday—I do not know what I am to do! I have decided not to part with the Burmese box, but everyone searcheth with great diligence and I am afeared that I shall be suspect, so I, too, do search alongside, the box under my arm. My armpit is sore!

'Friday—I have some luck at last! Mine good friend the innkeeper has agreed to hide the box in the tavern. I shall fetcheth it home when all is quiet.

'Monday—I have acted upon the good advice of mine friend the innkeeper and commenced upon the trade of opium. There is great profit in this. And I may travel much without fear or favour.

'Saturday—I have purchased much that is of great value, and gifted much also. But alack the day! Mine own kith and kin do take my gifts yet eye me with great suspicion. Mine heart is sore and I have determined to buy one mansion in the city.

'Sunday—I have discovered this secret space within this dome and I have kept this box and papers with great safety. Any jewels that remaineth will I give as gifts to mine kinsfolk. Here endeth mine journal. Sri Goja.'

Shejodadamoshai sighed as he reached the end of this remarkable piece of writing. 'I suppose Grandfather had the monkey-chasing ladder removed right after this. So Goja could no longer go and fetch things out of his box to present to others. He moved to Calcutta shortly after this and spent the rest of his life there. And now I understand why Podi-pishi chuckled just before she died. After all, in her opinion, no one but her darling Goja deserved the box and its contents, so she died happy!'

Everyone had been quiet so far. Now Khenti-pishi asked, 'What's in the box?'

Didima opened the cover, saying calmly, 'Whatever there is, *I'll* distribute it. Khenti, you still owe me three hundred rupees, but I'll give you this necklace.' Then she turned to Shejodadamoshai and said grimly, 'The less said about you, my dear brother-in-law, the better. However, this diamond ring is yours—This I'll give to my elder brother-in-law's son—This is for Panchu. Yes, he deserves something!—This is for Putki and this for Bunchki. And these are for me, I'll give them to my daughter.' She handed a pair of beautiful bangles to me to give to my mother. Then, in front of everyone, she kissed me and said, 'This emerald ring is left, and it's for you, my darling, because if you hadn't found the box, no one else would have! Now, let's go downstairs and have lunch. I've made a mountain of sweet coconut rolls for you. Oh, and by the way, I'm keeping the box; it'll do for my paan-masala.'

As I followed Didima out of the room, I heard Khenti-pishi snort and say to no one in particular, 'A queen's necklace for her, and I only get a single string! Hmmfff!'

And the skinny gentleman saying to Shejodadamoshai, 'Sir, what of my two hundred rupees?'

Goopy's Secret Diary

Chapter 1

It all happened a long, long time ago. So many years ago, in fact, that I thought I'd better write it all down, in case I forget any of the weird and wonderful happenings of that day.

There we were, four of us, crammed into one car: Thandidi, Shyamadas-kaka, Birinchi-da and I.

We drove on and on ... interminably, it seemed to me ... without stopping for anyone or anything. Didn't these people ever feel hungry or thirsty? Not that they hadn't come prepared, I reflected, looking at the enormous tiffin-carrier stuffed to the brim with fat mutton cutlets, poori and aloo-dum, crispy sweet sohan papri, just waiting to be eaten!

I was so hungry, my tummy had begun to make funny noises. After all, we had set out ever so early in the morning, hours before I usually get up. I had never woken up that early before. The crows hadn't started their morning arguments, those strange fellows who water the streets hadn't arrived, stars still twinkled faintly in a sky yet to turn blue, even Boggai hadn't woken up. He was fast asleep, sprawled at the foot of my bed, snoring loudly and twitching his tail in his dreams.

I missed Boggai! It would have been so comforting, so safe, to have him curled up quietly beside me. He wouldn't have done anyone any harm. But then, I hadn't planned all this.

Nobody should wake up so early! *I* didn't want to; in fact, I was just turning over and preparing to go back to sleep when I heard the noises: squeaks and scrapes, rattles and rustles, hushed whispers. As if the whole house was whispering, the trees outside were whispering, the whole world was whispering. How could I go to sleep with all that whispering going on around me?

Something strange was afoot, that's for sure, I thought. So I got up and crept out of my room to investigate. As I reached the landing outside my room, who should I see but Thandidi, wrapped in a large brown shawl, a very mysterious bundle under her arm, creeping downstairs, trying to walk as softly as her slippered feet would allow.

I raced after her and grabbed her from behind. Thandidi was so startled that she nearly fell down the steps. And that would have been the end of it! She would have brought down the roof and the whole household on us in a trice!

I asked, 'Where are you off to?'

Thandidi pulled herself together, clamped her cold hands over my mouth and hissed 'Shhhh!' Then she pointed down the stairs to the front door.

I stared. Two people were standing there, beckoning impatiently. One of them was my uncle, Shyamadas-kaka, and the other, our neighbour Birinchi-da. Both of them glared at me as I followed Thandidi downstairs. 'Why did you bring *him* along?' they demanded irritably. 'He'll spoil all our plans.'

'Okay, okay!' I retorted, with equal irritation. 'I'm going back to my room. And I'll tell Shejodadamoshai everything right away! . . . Shejo-dadu! Oy, Shejo-dadu—uu—uu . . .'

It worked like magic! They changed their tune instantly, almost falling over each other in their eagerness to please me. 'Don't, dear boy, don't yell like that. You'll have them all out in a trice! Why don't you come along with us, old fellow? You'll enjoy the drive . . . Look at all the goodies we have in that tiffin-carrier in the car . . . chops, cutlets, devilled eggs. But don't tell a soul!'

I turned to look. There, standing in front of the house, was Birinchi-da's ancient, ramshackle Ford, piled to the roof with luggage. Tucked inside the car was an enormous brass tiffin-carrier.

I looked up. The sky was fading to a pale, milky blue. Across its opalescent surface floated a thin, dark line of migratory birds and the rush and sweep of their wings came faintly to my ears—a wild, *calling* sound.

That decided me! I raced back upstairs, slipped on my new shoes, splashed some water on my face and combed my hair. Then I emptied my school bag of all junk and tucked in a spare set of clothes, my top, some string, a piece of broken mirror, my new comb and other useful articles. Then I shot downstairs and into the car. Ma-Baba were in Bombay, Putli was with them, so I didn't have to tell a soul. Otherwise I certainly wouldn't have been allowed to leave like this!

Birinchi-da was standing beside the car, looking impatiently at his watch every two seconds or so as if I had caused the delay. Huh, you asked me . . . no, *begged* me to go along. Then why this show of temper, now? Not that I didn't feel a wee bit nervous. What if we were stopped even before we could start off on our journey? There was Shejo-dadu to be reckoned with. Everyone said he always slept with one ear open, that he could even hear a mouse scurry past!

Luckily for us, no one woke up, no one came to find out what we were up to! I sat in the front—I never sit in the back seat unless I am forced to do so—beside my Shyamadas-kaka. He's a wonderful driver; didn't make a sound starting up that rattletrap Ford. It was Birinchi-da's car, but he's scared of cars, like many other things, and leaves the driving to Shyamadas-kaka.

It became obvious at once that this wasn't going to be a

short trip. We were heading straight out of Calcutta. The streets were empty at this time of the morning and a thin mist floated over the ground, giving everything a ghostly, unreal appearance. A cold breeze blew in through the open window of the car.

We were soon away from the sprawling expanse of the city. I watched as the sky lightened still further, and oddly enough, the western sky flushed red before the east turned pink and then crimson as the sun inched over the horizon. Cows began calling from their sheds, a few chicken came out and began to scratch in the dust, and the villagers began to wake up.

Inside the car, everyone was strangely silent. Of course, it may have been because Birinchi-da's car made so much noise in so many different ways that talking was next to impossible. You had to shout to be heard even by someone sitting next to you! But I somehow got the impression that these three were frightened of something . . . or some*one*. Once or twice I tried asking a few questions but was snapped at so irritably that I finally gave up any attempts at reasonable conversation. What was the use? Besides, *I* didn't care if they were frightened!

I was beginning to feel hungry. I hadn't had a very satisfying dinner last night. There had been that slight *contretemps* with Pishima for making glue in her best pan . . . and I had, unfortunately, come out the loser! It was well past breakfast time now, yet nobody said a word about food.

I was fidgeting about uncomfortably in my seat, when

Birinchi-da brought his mouth close to my ear and hissed, 'Sit quietly, can't you, boy? Look, just keep as quiet as a mouse for a while, and I'll give you a ... er ... some chewing gum. That's right, an enormous chewing gum.'

I gaped at him. This was most astonishing from someone who had never given anyone anything, no, not so much as a lizard's tail! What was *up*? No one wanted to explain anything, however, so I tried to sit still, my mind in a whirl.

On and on we went, speeding along the highway, the car eating up the miles easily despite its age and decrepit condition. It was broad daylight now and my tummy was beginning to demand attention in no uncertain terms, when I saw, some way ahead, a large crowd gathered under a massive tamarind tree near a level crossing.

What was it? An accident?

It was still quite far away, but I noticed that the trio in the car were alarmed, for some reason, especially Shyamadas-kaka. He had gripped the steering wheel so hard that his knuckles gleamed white. His hair was standing on end and there were large drops of perspiration all over his forehead. I looked again at the crowd. It really *was* unusually large. Something must have happened . . . something exciting, with accidents and blood, perhaps. When I turned to Shyamadas-kaka to ask him about it, he said sharply, without taking his eyes off the road, 'If you have nothing better to do, suck your thumb!'

I stared at him curiously. His voice sounded harsh and

unnatural. I noticed that the first few drops of sweat had joined together and trickled down in tiny streams, soaking the collar of his shirt, and new drops had taken their place on his furrowed brow.

By then we had reached the crowd near the level crossing. There seemed to be hundreds of people gathered under the massive tree, spilling over on to the road. A tea-seller with his little stove, copper kettle and basket of earthenware cups was sitting right beside the road, dangerously close to the passing car, but Shyamadas-kaka didn't notice him.

I looked back at the other two. Thandidi and Birinchi-da were sitting stiffly upright, their faces pale, their eyes like saucers. What on earth was the matter?

We had reached the level crossing, but here the crowd was so thick that, willy-nilly, Shyamadas-kaka had to stop the car. I stood up and looked out of the window, trying to see whether the accident victims were all in one piece or not. But I couldn't see a thing, no headless corpse, no head, nothing!

I looked at the tea-seller. He had a glass box filled with what I call 'monkey-biscuits'. They are so delicious . . . crisp and crunchy with a faintly nutty smell and coconut-ish taste. Wonderful! But I had no money.

I looked hopefully at the others, but they were still frozen with fear.

So I turned to look at the milling crowd. There seemed to be an extraordinary number of highly suspicious-looking people lurking among all the other more ordinary folk.

What was more, there were several policemen, too, carrying thick sticks and wearing smart blue turbans. Something was UP!

I stuck my head out of the window again and began to ask the nearest policeman: 'Here, constable, sir! What's happened?' But before I could utter a word, Birinchi-da and Thandidi pounced on me and dragged me back, while Shyamadas-kaka hissed, '*Idiot!*'

A thin, tall youth, with oily locks cut rather long, wearing lungi and a vest that had seen better days, had been glancing our way. Now he lounged forward and leaned casually against our car. He grinned at us with easy familiarity, showing red, paan-stained teeth, and I noticed that he wore tiny gold rings in his ears and that there was a daub of lime on his earlobe. Someone had told me once that if you did that, the lime in your paan wouldn't burn your mouth. Must try it out someday!

The young man said, 'Our zamindar-babu's wife's priceless pearl necklace has been stolen. That's why there are so many policemen out today.'

All this while the others had been sitting stiffly upright like puppets, their eyes staring straight ahead. Now they heaved a collective sigh of relief and began to chatter away with the oily-haired youth. Sitting beside the level crossing, under that tamarind tree, in that crowd, Shyamadas-kaka, Birinchi-da and Thandidi poured out a flood of information to the young stranger, while I listened in open-mouthed astonishment at things I had never even imagined, let alone known.

They said that we were driving down to Gaya to do the *pindadaan* puja for Thandidi's father, a puja done for the peace of the departed soul. (I didn't know Thandidi had a father. She's quite ancient herself!) Thandidi was to perform the puja, Birinchi-da was in charge of all the arrangements, Shyamadas-kaka was our driver and general bodyguard. As for me, I was Thandidi's precious grandson who couldn't stay away from her even for half a day. When I heard she was going away, I had created such a furore that they had had to take me along.

At this point, Thandidi patted me affectionately on the head, mussing up my hair. I had been so astonished at this spate of unknown information that so far I had forgotten to protest. Now I took out my little comb and bit of mirror and combed my hair smooth again. I hoped the old lady took the hint!

At that moment a white-uniformed inspector appeared, heading through the crowd towards us. Immediately the lungi-clad youth moved away from the car and melted into a group of people nearby. Shyamadas-kaka began to honk the horn with a great show of impatience, while the other two looked around at the crowd, as if nothing had happened.

The inspector came up to the car and spoke a few words to Shyamadas-kaka, who offered him a cigarette. The two lighted up, then the inspector said, 'Okay!' and the crowd parted as if by magic. The car surged forward, bounced across the railway tracks and we headed out along the highway once more.

I couldn't bear it any longer. Leaning forward, I grabbed hold of Shyamadas-kaka's hand, almost pulling it off the steering wheel. 'Tell me why all three of you are running away?' I demanded.

Shyamadas-kaka jumped and dropped his hands from the wheel, and the car careened across the road with a sickening lurch. My uncle grabbed hold and steadied the car, then turned to gape at me, open-mouthed at the unexpected question.

But it was Thandidi who answered from the back seat, her voice as harsh as a corncrake's. 'We *have* to run away! There's a *huliya* out for us!'

Chapter 2

A *huliya* after us! Oh my gosh and golly!

I edged along the seat, to get as close to Shyamadas-kaka as possible. He grunted, 'Ouf! Move up, move up, you're almost sitting on the gears!'

Birinchi-da added his two bits. In a grim voice he said, 'We're runaways! Exiles! We're leaving home and hearth forever. Happy now, you pest of a boy? Bothering us with questions ever since we started out!'

Thandidi sat forward. 'Oh no, not forever,' she exclaimed anxiously. 'We can't be exiles forever. The boy has his annual exams in December, remember? We have to return in good time for that. Also, I've left my paan-masala box behind, and I can't do without it.'

There was a tense silence in the car.

Do *huliyas* bite?

The road was becoming more deserted with each passing mile. There had been villages and farmland at first; now there was nothing but trees and some open land. Tall old banyans and tamarinds grew on either side of the road, their massive branches meeting overhead, intertwining to form a roof over us. It was as if we were driving through a green tunnel.

It was terribly lonely and quiet now. So quiet that even during midday, and sitting in that noisy car, I could hear the sound of a million crickets among the trees. The sound made you drowsy. Sometimes it seemed as though the crickets were very close; then they seemed to move miles away.

I was almost dropping off when Shyamadas-kaka drew to a halt on one side of the road and sat back, panting heavily. I knelt up on my seat and turned to face Thandidi. 'Why did you tell that fellow a pack of lies?' I said accusingly. 'Why did you say I'd howled my head off to come with you? You forced me to come along, just in case I told Shejo-dadu everything. You *bribed* me with cutlets and chewing gum, didn't you?'

They answered in one voice, 'Tell your Shejo-dadu— what? What do *you* know to tell him?'

They were right, of course. What did I know of this mysterious trip? Crushed, I sat back, pulled out the tin frog from my pocket and began to rattle it softly. This seemed to relieve the others; they sat back, too, and wiped their foreheads. Shyamadas-kaka thrust his hand in his pocket to take out a hanky . . . and jumped nearly out of his skin!

'Birinchi, just put your hand in my pocket and see if what I felt there is really it!'

Birinchi-da gaped; then he leaned over the seat and thrust his hand in Shyamadas-kaka's pocket, scrabbled about for a minute—and drew forth a stunning string of pearls! We stared at the jewel, open-mouthed. They looked just like the pearls described in the fairy tales: round and lustrous, like frozen tears. They glowed in the sunshine, sending out rainbow colours.

Rivers of blood have flowed for such things!

Thandidi gasped, '*Shyamadas*! Oh Shyamadas, I didn't think you had it in you!'

Birinchi-da added, in tones of reluctant admiration, 'My goodness, Shyamadas, you really *are* something! But what astonishes me is how and when you managed this sleight of hand!'

I couldn't help sniggering. 'Shyamadas-kaka steal something like this! Hah! He's scared of cockroaches, creepy-crawlies give him the willies—and *he* commit a desperate crime! No way! Do you know what I think has happened? That lungi-clad fellow slipped it into his pocket when he was leaning against the car. He's the thief, and he was afraid the police would search him and so . . .'

Thandidi shivered. 'The boy's right! Oh Shyamadas, wipe it with your hanky, quick. Your fingerprints are all over it.'

'Now we'll see who protects you from the law,' said Birinchi-da maliciously. 'They'll set a whole horde of detectives after you. And even if you do escape them, that oily youth will be after you to get it back. There'll be murder and mayhem, and bloodshed and . . .'

At this point, I noticed a change in Shyamadas-kaka's appearance. His eyes had narrowed; the colour of his face and even the shape of his ears had changed. I don't think he really wanted to give up the necklace. He slipped it into his pocket and started the car without saying another word.

Birinchi-da suddenly glanced over his shoulder and exclaimed, 'Oh my goodness! Shyamadas, I think there's a car after us!'

Shyamadas-kaka reacted as though he had been stung. He swerved off the road and headed straight into the trees. There was a narrow but well-defined pathway across the hummocks and tussocks, weaving in and out through the undergrowth and the trees. Shyamadas-kaka drove down this as easily as though he was driving along the highway.

Thandidi and Birinchi-da didn't protest. As for me, I was so hungry, I couldn't say a word. Nothing seemed worthwhile to me just then, except to fulfil the demands of my tummy! Once or twice I tried to ask meekly, 'Aren't you going to eat today?'

At first I was ignored. So I tried again, 'May I eat?'

This time Thandidi glared at me. 'Eat, eat, eat! Is that all you can think of?' she snapped. 'Haven't you been told that there's a *huliya* out for us!'

'What is a *huliya*?'

Birinchi-da said irritably, 'Don't be stupid, boy! As if you don't know what a *huliya* is! Wait until it catches up with you . . . then you won't have a chance to ask any questions.'

I looked out of the window. All around were tall trees, thick underbrush, occasional bare patches with outcrops of black rock; here and there the rough, red ground had broken away, showing twisted chewed-up roots of trees. It was all very wild and mysterious. *Hoondars* have their lairs in places like this . . . although everyone says they don't exist! They do, I'm sure of it. They drag their kill here . . . small goats and such-like animals, and they don't say no to small humans, either!

I suddenly realized that the door on my side wasn't properly shut . . . something wrong with the lock, I suppose. I slid along the seat towards Shyamadas-kaka and he snapped at me again. 'How many times have I told you not to press against the gears? Shove up.'

'Why are you driving so slowly? Suppose the door swings open and something jumps in?'

Shyamadas-kaka promptly stopped the car and glared at me. 'Right! Since you know so much, *you* do the driving,' he said. 'Can't you see the condition of the road

57

we're driving along? Is it fit for driving, eh? Let's change seats, then; come on!'

By then the road had narrowed to a mere footpath. The trees had crowded close about us, and the sound of the crickets ... believe it or not! ... nearly deafened us. It made you feel at once sleepy and sad. And I was so hungry! I took out my tin frog again, to help me take my mind off food.

Shyamadas-kaka seemed satisfied and set off again, but after a while he stopped under an enormous banyan tree. As soon as the engine was switched off, the silence of the forest surged over us. The only sounds were the rustle and whisper of the breeze through a million leaves, the interminable sound of the crickets, and from somewhere not far off, the tinkle and splash of falling water.

Hoondars come to places like this to quench their thirst! You can see their pugmarks in the wet sand beside the pool, and the marks where they have dragged their prey along.

Ooohhh, I was so hungry.

Then Shyamadas-kaka got out of the car, stretched and exclaimed, 'Let's eat. I'm famished!'

Thank goodness!

Birinchi-da looked at me. 'Come on, get up,' he said. 'Open the tiffin-carrier and get out the food. And there's water in that flask. Hurry up, hurry up! Oohh, my hands and feet are still wobbly, and there's a funny feeling in the pit of my tummy. Look sharp, my lad!'

I did hurry!

There was poori and aloo-dum, minced meat cutlets and

sweets. No devilled eggs or sohan papri, but what did it matter? This was good enough! I found some old newspapers in the car and served the food on those, since we didn't have any dishes. Shyamadas-kaka ate about twenty pooris; as for Birinchi-da, his fear seemed to have increased his appetite. Only Thandidi turned up her nose at the food and moved to one side; she made do with some fruits and sweets.

Strangely enough, none of the others seemed in the least happy. I was the only one who relished the feast spread out before us. After the meal, I drank some water, then dug around in my pocket and finally unearthed a lozenge (rather hairy after its long residence there with various other useful items). I popped it in my mouth, drew a long breath of contentment and said, 'Aaahhh, that was good!'

Immediately the other three were up in arms. 'Good!' they snapped. 'What's "good" about it all, hey? Have you given a thought to our situation? A deep, dark forest in front of us, enemies behind us, evening closing in! Soon it'll be dark, and *then* what are we to do?'

I couldn't help saying, 'Well, if Shyamadas-kaka hadn't driven into the jungle, we would have been . . .'

At which point Thandidi uttered a piercing shriek of 'Tiger! Help, tiger!' and leapt into the car with surprising agility, considering her age. I hastily followed suit. Then, having carefully locked the door, I looked out eagerly. No tiger! Instead I noticed a buffalo-type animal coming slowly through the forest. Birinchi-da shooed it away, and it lumbered off again.

Really, females are such scaredy-cats!

I got out of the car and looked around. A large toad hopped past me and squeezed itself into a crack under a rock nearby. For a long time after that, I watched its tiny eyes, twinkling in the dark. But I wasn't in the least scared, and I didn't tell Thandidi. Suppose she fainted or something! You never can tell with females!

Then Birinchi-da wiped his hands with his handkerchief, popped a paan in his mouth and said, 'Well, let's have a look at the marvellous necklace.' Shyamadas-kaka took it out of his pocket somewhat reluctantly, I thought.

'Wow, Shyamadas. If you aren't caught, you'll become a millionaire overnight, my lad. And if the police *do* get you . . . and that seems most likely . . . you'll have to spend the rest of your life in rigorous imprisonment.'

I felt excited. It would be interesting to have a criminal for an uncle! 'I know, I know!' I yelled. 'They tie coconut-shell goggles over your eyes, then harness you to an oil-press, and you have to go round and round, but you don't feel giddy, because your eyes are covered. And then . . .'

I had to stop, for Shyamadas-kaka suddenly gave me a stinging slap; then he snatched the necklace and flung it as far away from him as he could. The pearls glowed like a row of lamps on the green grass. Birinchi-da picked it up almost reverently. As I rubbed my smarting cheeks, I noticed for the first time a diamond locket hanging from the necklace.

It'll serve Shyamadas-kaka right if the *huliya* catches him, I thought. But then who'll drive the car?

Chapter 3

I looked all around.

The enormous banyan curved over us like a mammoth green umbrella. Some of the aerial roots hung down, waving to and fro in the breeze like withered brown fingers. Sunlight came through the leaves, dappling the forest floor and everything else with a greenish-gold light. A faint breeze shivered the branches and the leaves, whispering and murmuring through the forest.

Shyamadas-kaka snatched the necklace away from Birinchi-da and thrust it back into his pocket. 'I really am not bothered with such trifles,' he said with lofty solemnity. 'This necklace is hardly worth anything, you know, Birinchi, compared to what we had! Do you know, my grandmother used to wear jewellery worth a lakh of rupees in the morning, and in the evening, three lakhs! She had so many pieces of jewellery that she lost count of them. Sometimes, when another lady came to visit her, she would think that the visitor was wearing jewels that had been stolen from her collection—and she never hesitated to express her opinions, either. She made so many enemies that way. And that was what finished her!'

I had been listening in breathless silence. Now, as Shyamadas-kaka paused, I asked, 'Why? What happened?'

'Don't interrupt,' snapped my uncle. 'And don't rush me. I like to tell a tale at my own pace . . . Yes, well, she was stunningly beautiful, was my grandmother. Any other woman standing beside her looked like a monkey! Complexion like milk-and-roses, masses of curly dark hair that fell almost to her ankles, sparkling doe eyes, pearly teeth Oh, I could go on forever! And she used to go to bed at night wearing all those priceless jewels!'

'Then what happened?' I just had to ask. 'Something nasty, I'm sure.'

Shyamadas-kaka ignored me and continued, 'One morning she woke up to find every piece of jewellery she possessed had been stolen. She had no dearth of enemies, you see, thanks to her beauty and wealth and her imperious ways. It was the work of one such jealous enemy, of course. Someone had crept into her room at night and stolen everything she was wearing. But Grandmother didn't feel a thing!

'It was only when she woke up in the morning and was absent-mindedly scratching her arm that she realized that her armlet was missing. Then she saw that not only the gold armlet but every bit of jewellery she had on when she went to bed the previous night was missing: the diamond bracelets, turquoise-studded anklets, emerald necklace—everything! The thief had even picked off her diamond nose-stud.'

Shyamadas-kaka sighed lugubriously. 'Poor Grandmother! And you know what, I have a very strong feeling that this necklace . . . this paltry pearl chain . . . was one of those stolen jewels! I have no proof, of course, no one had ever made a list of what she possessed. In any case, most of the other jewels were worth lakhs; this one can't be much more than twenty thousand rupees.'

Birinchi-da leaned towards him. 'Shyamadas, beware!' he said, in the voice of doom. 'Greed has entered your soul. You know full well that this has nothing to do with your grandmother. This necklace belongs to that zamindar's wife. Perhaps you were hand in glove with that lungi-clad fellow . . . Be careful, or you'll hang for it!' I noticed that his face had turned green with envy.

Shyamadas-kaka scowled. He yelled in furious tones, 'What d'you mean? Why should I hang for it? Why should I hang for *anything*, for that matter? What about you and Pishima? After all, you two . . .'

Birinchi-da hastily covered his mouth with his hands and jerked his nose towards me. '*Hsshh*! Shush, old fellow! You never know who'll hear what! Calm down, please. Didn't I promise to take you out for dinner one day to the best Chinese restaurant in town?' He paused, then added, 'In any case, *you're* also in it . . . neck-deep. You can't deny that!'

Everyone fell silent after that.

Thandidi had remained in the car ever since she spotted the so-called tiger. Now she climbed out and uttered a small sigh. 'Hare Krishna, my Lord! Everything happens only according to Your wish! Else why should my poor Shejo-pishima's priceless pearl necklace vanish so mysteriously from her strongbox? Just imagine, there stood the heavy iron box under Shejo-pishima's bed, locked and tied up with a thick rope, dozens of heavy pots and pans piled on top of it. Shejo-pishima herself, perched on the bed, refusing to stir a step, waiting to present me with that necklace on my wedding day. And I wasn't even born then!

'And then one day, when she pulled everything out to check that her precious jewel was safe, she saw that it had gone . . . vanished! The rope was still wound round the strongbox, the pots and pans were in place, everything was as it should be. Only the precious necklace had gone! The shock killed her, and I never got to see the poor lady. Yet she wasn't too old . . . only eighty-one. Her mother and sisters lived up to ninety-seven or ninety-eight; she could easily have done so. This necklace . . . it looks exactly like that one!' Thandidi paused, then added, 'In a manner of speaking, this necklace actually belongs to *me*.'

Birinchi-da was not to be outdone. 'D'you think such necklaces haven't come into my life! Well, just listen to this . . . every word absolutely true! The first time I sat for my B.A. exams, I was just entering the examination hall on the very last day, when a sadhu came up to me, palms outstretched, begging for alms. I had very little money with me, except the couple of rupees I had been given for my tram fare; I had to give that, you can't turn a sadhu away empty-handed, you know. Especially before an exam!

'The sadhu beamed at me, patted my head and said, "Well, young man, even the Goddess of Wisdom and Learning won't be able to make you pass your exams, so no point giving you my blessings to that effect! However, keep this: you might find it of some help later on." And he handed me a small bundle. Later that evening, when I got home, I opened the bundle and saw . . . a pearl necklace, exactly like this one!'

'Where is it, then?' I asked eagerly.

Birinchi-da sighed deeply. 'Lost! That's the tragedy of it all! I had put the bundle in the pocket of my pants, and absent-mindedly sent it off to the cleaners without taking it out. Well, washermen don't return so much as a pencil; would they return such a thing as that? The washerman vanished, too, the very next day! I don't suppose you'll believe me, but every word is true!'

I decided that I had to say something, too. 'Oh yes, I remember something, too,' I began.

The three of them turned on me as one. 'Shut up! Don't make things up!'

Thandidi sighed again and said, 'Whenever I think of that necklace, I get goose bumps! Remember the time when there was that pandemonium in the zoo, after the tiger took fright at a lady's feathery hat and escaped from his cage? Everyone in the city locked their doors and windows and stayed indoors, preferably on the top floor, for days. Don't you remember? . . . Oh, silly me! You weren't even born then! . . . My goodness! What terrifying days they were! Yet my poor dear Shejo-pishima didn't give up her post even for a minute. How sad the necklace should vanish in that way! How sad!' And Thandidi sniffed and wiped her eyes with the corner of her sari.

Shyamadas-kaka looked irritated. 'Keep your emotions

under check for the time being,' he said sharply. 'We haven't any time for all that. We'll have to decide what to do next.'

Thandidi scowled. 'Yes, I can read between the lines! You have no intention of giving up that necklace, do you? Very well, let's do something, then. Come on, get in the car, everyone, and let's go.'

'What do you mean . . . let's go?' said Shyamadas-kaka, somewhat taken aback. 'Let me tell you that that car won't go an inch further. There isn't a drop of petrol in its tanks, all its tyres are punctured, and for the past hour or so it's been making a most peculiar groaning sound. I don't like it!'

It was Birinchi-da's turn to get annoyed. He went scarlet in the face and stuttered, 'Wh . . . what d'you mum . . . mean—all the tut . . . tyres are punctured? Have you any idea how expensive they are? And what about that groaning, eh? That wasn't there before, was it?'

Shyamadas-kaka ignored him and went on, 'In any case, the track ends here. No self-respecting car could go any further. Now, what are we to do?'

All three of them looked at me. I cleared my throat. 'Let's go and look for some kind of shelter for the night, shall we?' I said. 'We can give a final shape to our plot there.'

'Plot? What do you mean "plot"?' exclaimed Thandidi, annoyed. 'Where do you learn such things? . . . In any case, we can't wander about this forest with that priceless necklace. Or go looking for shelter with complete strangers!'

I got up. 'Right! Then you stay here, I'm off!' I said. 'Stay inside the car, if you like, but don't blame *me* if you're all eaten by a *hoondar*. One more thing: isn't a *huliya* out after you?'

That did the trick!

Instantly, they all tumbled out of the car, trampling on each other's toes, pushing and shoving to get out as fast as possible. Then they looked at me.

I stretched myself thankfully, for I was stiff with sitting still for so long. I flexed my arms and legs and hopped about for a bit, just as Baba had shown me, to get rid of the cramps. The other three gaped at me.

'What on earth are you up to?' Birinchi-da exclaimed after a while. 'Stop all that rubbish and lock up the car. Don't forget to roll up the windows. I'd do it myself, but I've got the cramps, too.'

I scrabbled around in the tiffin-carrier for any leftover food, stuffing a few pooris and cutlets into my pocket. As I began to roll up the window, Shyamadas-kaka said, 'And one more thing: just keep this necklace with you. I'm so absent-minded, I'll be sure to lose it.' And he thrust the beautiful thing into my hand.

I grinned as I rolled up the last window, the necklace still clutched in my hand. The pearls glimmered in the twinkling starlight. And then . . . and then . . . Oh my goodness!

What shouldn't have happened did happen!

Disaster!

Yet I couldn't tell a soul! And no one noticed anything, either. So I just kept quiet about it . . . for the time being.

Chapter 4

What a forest!

It was already dark under the thousands of trees that clustered thickly together. In the clearing by the stream, the afterglow of late evening had given us some light. Once we entered the forest proper, that was shut off. Millions of leaves, fed and fattened by thousands of years of monsoon rains, blocked even the least glimmer of light. To top it all, it began to rain. The drops pattered on the treetops, dripped steadily down twig by twig, leaf by leaf, and then on to us. It was bitterly cold!

Underfoot, a carpet of withered and decaying leaves deadened all sounds. Only when someone stepped on a dry branch, the crack echoed through the forest like a rifle shot, shattering the silence to a thousand pieces and making everyone jump in fright. Otherwise, it was so quiet, we might as well have been deaf.

We went in single file, slowly, head hanging down, everyone labouring under a deep sense of anxiety. As for me, I didn't know what to do. The disaster that had taken place a few minutes ago filled me with foreboding. And yet I couldn't tell anyone; I had to bear the burden alone!

Down the narrow forest track we went, keeping as close

as we could to each other, partly because of the cold, mostly through fear. Nobody had a torch, of course . . . one never does when one needs it the most! So we stumbled on through the pitch darkness, feeling our way as we went, like so many blind men.

I began to feel hungry again. I suddenly remembered the pooris in my pocket, and slipped my hand in to feel them. They had become a greasy lump; they shouldn't be kept for long, I thought. As I began to pull them out I saw, not far ahead, a light shining through the trees.

A light! That meant people . . . shelter . . . and, most important of all, food!

I didn't waste a second, but stuffed the pooris into my mouth and began to chomp on them for all I was worth! I hate wasting anything in the food line, you see. But what an awful racket! That chewing, chomping sound echoed round and round the silent forest until even the trees seemed to shudder in disgust.

My companions jumped nearly out of their skins. 'What's happened? What's up?'

I swallowed my mouthful, nearly choking in the process, and managed to croak, 'Look! A light!'

What excitement, then! And what a change in their attitude! All this while they had been trudging along, heads bowed, shoulders hunched against the rain, the picture of misery. Now they straightened their backs and shoulders and marched forth briskly . . . so briskly, that in a short while we had reached the source of light.

It was a huge, crumbling mansion set in a clearing in the forest. At one time it must have been painted grey, but now the paint was peeling off from the walls and bricks showed here and there, giving the house a horrible scabby, diseased appearance. Most of the shutters hung crazily on their hinges; some had disappeared altogether. Bushes and weeds grew in the cracks, and the whole edifice looked as though it would crumble to dust at any moment. But at least it was shelter of a sort!

The front door, a massive affair and still very sturdy, was shut. However, through the cracks in the shuttered window on one side of the porch, chinks of light could be seen— the lights we had seen through the trees.

So there *was* someone inside the house!

Birinchi-da stepped up to the door and tapped softly. The rest of us huddled together under the porch, away from the rain, breathing heavily down each other's necks.

There was no sound.

Then Shyamadas-kaka pushed Birinchi-da aside and banged so hard on the door that the old shutters and broken doors rattled loudly. We looked around in alarm but there was no one there. I looked up . . . and it seemed that several people were watching us intently through the cracks of a shuttered window above the porch. I moved away quickly.

Shyamadas-kaka banged again and again and after a while we heard a soft, heavy tread coming towards the door. I shrank closer to my uncle, my heart thumping! I thought, why on earth did we come here? We could very well have spent the night in the car and decided on the best course of action tomorrow morning. That would have been much safer.

Just at that moment there was a sharp click and a small square opening appeared in the centre panel of the door. Then a beady black eye, surmounted by a wild bush of an eyebrow, surveyed us suspiciously.

Thandidi stepped forward. 'We aren't thieves or robbers, or any such things,' she called. 'We're just a group of weary travellers, hungry and thirsty, looking for some shelter. Just open the door and let us in, please.'

There was a moment's tense silence. Then, slowly, the eye withdrew and the small opening shut with a click. After a while, we heard the sound of innumerable keys being turned in rusty locks, bolts being opened and chains shifted. It took nearly ten minutes, then the door opened slowly.

We didn't wait a second but almost fell inside through the doorway.

We found ourselves in a huge room, paved with uneven stone tiles. The peeling walls were uneven, too, and the shadows cast by a flickering oil lamp placed on a wobbly three-legged stool leaped and jumped across them. On one side there was a massive flight of wooden steps leading upstairs.

Standing in the middle of the room was an immensely tall old lady, her hair tied in a topknot, an enormous ladle in her hand. Wafting all about her was the mouth-watering fragrance of hot khichri.

We huddled together in the middle of the room, soaking wet, hungry and scared. The water dripped off our clothes and hair and streamed across the floor in tiny rivulets, to gather in a puddle about our feet. The old lady looked at the mess with an air of gloomy resignation. But she didn't utter a word. Perhaps she wasn't a Bengali, and couldn't understand the language.

Shyamadas-kaka seemed to have come to the same conclusion. He stepped forward, raised his voice and said in a mixture of Hindi and Bengali, speaking slowly, 'We no bad people! We good! We much hungry, much muddy, much wet . . .'

The old lady opened her mouth. 'Okay, okay, young man!' she exclaimed, in a sort of muted roar. 'That's enough! What I am wondering is . . . how on earth am I to feed and clothe so many of you at such short notice?'

'We won't need anything much,' said Shyamadas-kaka pleadingly. 'A couple of old towels will do for us; we can even dry ourselves with an old shirt or something.'

Thandidi put in her two bits, 'I won't need anything, my child. I can't use just anybody's old cloth to dry my hair . . . goodness knows *where* it's been! My sari is good enough for me. All we need is shelter for the night.'

We all looked appealingly at the old woman; she stared back with a thunderous expression on her face. Just at that moment we heard, quite distinctly, the sound of knocking somewhere in the distance. All of us jumped nearly out of our skins. As for the old lady, she slipped, eel-like, out of the room through the back door before any one of us could do or say a thing.

Well, we stood there, each in our own individual puddle, wondering who else could have been wandering around the forest on this stormy night and feeling mighty uncomfortable about the whole affair.

Could it be . . . could it be the dreaded . . . *huliya*! I felt my heart beginning to beat much too fast for comfort. But did the *huliya*, whatever they were, announce their arrival by such thunderous knocks? I would have thought that they would creep silently after their prey, from bush to shadow. And then, at an opportune moment, they would spring out and . . .

The sound of a door opening and shutting echoed through the silent house. We held our breaths and strained our ears to catch the least sound—and we heard the old woman talking to somebody in a hoarse whisper. Then that sound, too, faded away, and we were left to wait in the shadowed room, while the only sound was the ceaseless dripping of the rain and the loud flapping of the wings of some butterfly-like creature that fluttered and swooped around the lamp.

Then the old woman returned.

But what a change in her! Gone was the stormy expression; instead she beamed at us as though we were her favourite relatives. It was quite scary, really.

Rubbing her hands together in a great show of servility, she exclaimed, 'Oh yes, what was I saying? Yes. What an honour to have such guests in my poor hovel! Please come this way. I will take you upstairs, yes, of course. There are dry towels for all of you, and dry clothes, too, if you would care for them . . . Don't worry, madam, I have clean new towels for you to use . . . no one has touched them. And, yes, please deign to eat whatever poor food I have cooked tonight, if you don't mind. I shall be highly honoured . . . ' etc. etc.

I kept on thinking, this is highly suspicious; why on earth did we come here? We'd have been better off in the car. Still, there was nothing for it now, but to follow the old lady upstairs.

The wooden staircase was covered with centuries-old dust. Most of the steps creaked like a convention of crickets, some were so worm-eaten as to be really dangerous, and in many places the handrails had disappeared. Still, it must once have been a magnificent flight of stairs.

Upstairs, this feeling of decaying splendour persisted. The rooms were all enormous with wooden floors that hadn't been polished for years and the faded remnant of once brilliant murals still visible on the walls. In the flickering light of the lamp, the painted deer and their hunters seemed to be alive. I shivered, feeling suddenly cold.

The creaky wooden floors were as dusty as the staircase, and with each footstep we sent up a puff of soft, grey dust, like smoke signals. These rooms had obviously been uninhabited for years.

One room in the front, however, had been cleaned and

made suitable for use. There were four massive wooden divans with ornate, carved legs, and an ancient table with equally ornate legs set in a corner . . . and that was all. The old lady set the lamp in a sort of niche in the wall and showed us the bathroom next door. She herself fetched a bucket of hot water for us to wash and, as promised, four clean towels and four sets of clothes, smelling pleasantly of soap and sun-warmed grass. We were astonished! How on earth had she managed to produce all these things in a crumbling mansion in the middle of the forest?

To top it all, within an hour, the old lady brought up four large dishes filled with steaming, fragrant khichri and mutton curry. They were superbly cooked! Thandidi, of course, refused to eat anything; no problem,we three polished off her share! I felt rather sad for poor Thandidi.

'Would you like some chewing gum?' I asked, thinking that perhaps she was hungry.

Thandidi wrinkled her nose. 'No, thank you, my child,' she sniffed. 'I don't touch those things, made with eggs!'

Dinner over, the old lady cleared away the dishes and brought up four rugs and four small pillows. All of us were so tired that we stretched out at once. Nobody wanted to waste any more time in useless speculation, although all of us were highly suspicious about how the old lady managed to provide these homely comforts. Anyway, we were too tired to keep awake much longer. In a very short time, the other three, at least, were fast asleep.

For some reason, however, I couldn't go to sleep. I lay, tossing and turning, listening to the incredible number of sounds that could be heard in that silent old house.

It was raining still, raindrops falling on the treetops, dripping down from the eaves, beating against a tin roof somewhere, splattering on the floor of our room as the rain was blown in through the window by the wind. And the wind itself made so many sounds . . . swishing through branches of the trees, rattling the doors and shutters, whistling through chinks and cracks.

I heard the sound of pots and pans being washed, probably by the old lady. Once I even thought I heard a cow moo.

A cow! Here, in the middle of the forest!

It was too much for me. I slipped out of bed and padded over to the window on the far side of the room. It overlooked a sort of yard behind the house. Through a gap in the shutters I saw a tin shed on the other side of a courtyard. A small lamp burned there, and in its flickering, uncertain light I saw a small, rather meek-looking old man with a scrubby beard milking an enormous cow that looked extremely ferocious and decidedly carnivorous!

Now, who on earth would require so much milk in the middle of the night, I thought. But at least it showed there were other people in the house. Somehow, the thought was comforting. Then, as I turned away from the window, my blood turned cold.

Someone was silently shutting the door of our room.

Chapter 5

I don't know how long I stood rooted to the spot, my ears buzzing. That sound wasn't crickets, I thought; it was the sound of my blood rushing through my veins. I strained to catch any other sounds . . . the least little suspicious noise . . . but all I could hear was the sound of the wind rustling through the leaves, the incessant drip and thrum of the rain and the deep breathing of the other three. They must be really fast asleep!

I pushed the thought of the pearl necklace to the back of my mind. No, I wouldn't think of it. Strangely enough, the others seemed to have pushed it to the backs of their minds easily enough. They hadn't said a word about it ever since Shyamadas-kaka handed it to me; and yet they had been so petrified about it only a few hours ago. Now they were deeply and comfortably asleep, snoring their heads off. Weird!

I went back to bed. As I lay down, the big, solid-looking divan creaked alarmingly, but no one stirred. Neither did they move a muscle when I took out my precious chewing gum and unwrapped it with an inevitably loud crackle that made me start. I popped a piece into my mouth, folded the remaining in the wrapper and slipped it into my pocket, which was stained with the oily pooris I had kept there earlier in the day. I wiped my greasy fingers on my hair and lay back, thinking over the events of the day.

Neither Shyamadas-kaka nor Birinchi-da were great travellers; as for Thandidi, she rarely stepped out of the house. Yet look at them now, I thought. Miles from Calcutta, in a crumbling house in the middle of nowhere. And sleeping as peacefully as though they were safely in their own comfortable beds at home.

I suddenly remembered the *huliya*. Had we managed to shake it off, or was it still on our trail? Goodness only knew where it was, or what it was up to. Perhaps it would sniff us out and arrive at this old house with a roar and a snarl!

I nearly swallowed my chewing gum in fright, but just managed to stop it slipping down my throat at the last moment. Oohh, that was a close shave, I thought, tucking the precious piece behind my teeth. I'd have to make it last the night ... and it looked like being a very long night, too.

I turned over, wondering how the *huliya* had managed to sniff out all these people at one go. I mean, it wasn't as though they all lived in the same place. Birinchi-da did live next door, but Shyamadas-kaka had his own house in Shyambazar. He wasn't much of an uncle, true, but he was a super driver, and knew everything about cars and their workings. But he and I never got on very well together. As for Birinchi-da—well, he was rich and pampered ... even had servants to take off his shoes for him! Also he had a huge house and plenty of cars. Yet he didn't drive. The reason for that, he had told me once, was that he had run over someone years ago and had been hauled off to the police station. Since that day he had refused to touch another steering wheel.

I had nearly dozed off, thinking about all this. The sound of blood rushing through my veins, the pitter-patter of raindrops, the sounds from the forest—all seemed to move far away, when I heard a faint creak of the wooden staircase. Instantly I was wide awake. I heard the sound again, as well as the scuff of bare feet moving with cat-like stealth somewhere just down the corridor. All the stories I had ever read or heard about robbers and murderers flashed through my mind. I lay frozen, my eyes closed to mere slits.

Thandidi and Birinchi-da still slept on, as unconcerned as ever. Only Shyamadas-kaka turned over to face the wall beside his bed and began to snore loudly. I knew then that he, at least, was awake.

The scuffling footsteps stopped outside our room. There was a moment's silence; then, very slowly and cautiously the door was pushed open, letting in a sliver of light. I nearly stopped breathing. Through half-shut eyes I saw the old man who had been milking the cow; he had disguised himself by tying a dirty hanky around the lower half of his face and in one hand he carried a lantern wrapped in black paper. Behind him was the lungi-clad youth we had seen at the level crossing that morning; he, too, had his face covered with a hanky. He bent over us, intently studying each face, and I noticed something in his hand that looked too much like a long thin dagger for my comfort!

After a long, breathless (on my part) moment, the two of them seemed convinced that we were really asleep. Then, soft-footed, they went across to Shyamadas-kaka's bed. So this is the end of my uncle, I thought. I forgave him all the trouble he had caused me all these years—the scolding and punishments, the jibes and jeers and sneaky attacks when I was least expecting them! I had to forgive him . . . his last moment had arrived.

Shyamadas-kaka snored on steadily. The oily youth proceeded to search him from head to foot, but they couldn't find the necklace. How could they? It was further away than anyone guessed! Having drawn a blank there, they turned their attention to Birinchi-da. Immediately Shyamadas-kaka's snores stopped and Birinchi-da began emitting the most realistic rumbles from his nose! However, he, too, proved to be necklace-less—naturally.

After this the old man went downstairs and fetched up the old woman to search Thandidi from head to foot. I think Thandidi really fainted with fright! In the meantime, the oily youth searched me, and I snored with great feeling all through. But of course they couldn't find the necklace on any one of us!

Finally, after a thorough search all around, they gave up. Disappointed, they trailed out of the room and shut the door as silently as they had opened it. The light disappeared and soon the soft footsteps died away, too. There were faint creaks and crunches on the stairs, then silence.

I suddenly realized that it had stopped raining. The only sound now was the steady drip-drip-drip from the leaves and from the parapets above the windows, and the mournful hoot of a sodden barn owl. I lay still, my heart beating very fast, completely awake by now.

After a long while, I heard Birinchi-da whisper to Shyamadas-kaka, 'Where did you manage to hide the thing?'

Shyamadas-kaka sat up. 'I didn't hide it,' he said. 'In fact, I gave it to Goopy to keep. Here Goopy, where is it?'

I kept quiet. I had nothing to say.

Shyamadas-kaka gave a snort of annoyance. 'Hey, cat got your tongue? Give me that necklace, I say. After all, it came to me, you might say, so it belongs to *me*.' Then he heaved a sigh of relief. 'Well, that's that, then. Now I can be easy in my mind about it. As soon as it is light, I'll walk down to the nearest rail station. Then off to Calcutta! Goopy, hand over my necklace.'

Thandidi glared at him. 'What do you mean *your* necklace?' she demanded indignantly. 'You know very well it belongs to the wife of the zamindar here . . . and it's stolen property! Okay, go to Calcutta . . . then just you wait and see what I do to you.'

Shyamadas-kaka ignored her and gave me a little push. 'Goopy, give me the necklace.'

'I don't have the necklace with me,' I said.

'What d'you mean, you don't have it?' exclaimed Birinchi-da. 'Of course you do! Take it out of your pocket.'

'I don't have it, I tell you,' I cried. 'If you don't believe me, you can search me.'

That's exactly what they did. Growling with annoyance, Shyamadas-kaka and Birinchi-da searched me from head to foot. Then they lit matches and searched the whole room, but drew a blank! When Birinchi-da had used up every last stick in his matchbox, Shyamadas-kaka thrust his hand into his pocket to take out his box . . . and jumped nearly out of his skin!

'Birinchi,' he said, in a hoarse whisper, 'just put your hand in my pocket and see if what I thought is there, is really there!'

Birinchi-da complied at once; he put his hand inside Shyamadas-kaka's pocket and took out *another* pearl necklace! In the quivering light of the matchstick, the pearls glowed like small moons. I gaped. Then I blinked, pinched myself, blinked again. Was I awake or dreaming? How could the necklace be in Shyamadas-kaka's pocket, when . . .? No, no, impossible!

I gasped, 'Let me have a look!'

By then it had stopped raining. The gusty wind had driven away the clouds and the moon shone out of a clear, starry sky. The room was illuminated by the pale silver gleam, and I stared at the beautiful thing in Birinchi-da's hand. The pearls glowed with a fiery lustre that was quite dazzling.

But . . . it *couldn't* be the same necklace! No one knew that better than I did. I looked closely at it. Yes, it was similar but not the same. There were differences: the other one had a huge diamond pendant, this one had a sapphire hung from it.

I said earnestly, 'It's not the same necklace. I tell you, this is a different one!'

Shyamadas-kaka glared at me. 'Very well, give me the other one, then. All the better for me . . . I'll have two valuable pieces of jewellery. Come on, Goopy, hand over the other one.'

I hung my head and kept quiet. What *could* I say? Instead, I took a piece of chewing gum and popped it into my mouth.

Thandidi put in her two bits. 'I knew it would come to all this,' she said with a sniff. 'Godless people, never saying your daily prayers or performing any sort of puja. In fact, that Birinchi goes so far as to say that . . .'

'Why drag all that in, now?' Birinchi-da interrupted hastily. 'This isn't the time and place for it.'

Thandidi was not to be put off. 'Don't you see, we're being dogged by misfortune,' she sniffled. 'Otherwise, how would you explain the fact that we've had so many setbacks since the morning, and we haven't yet reached our destination? We took all precautions, made all the arrangements, and yet we failed on all counts. Now, the Lord only knows what will happen.'

'Don't say that,' said Birinchi-da anxiously, while Shyamadas-kaka fidgeted uncomfortably. 'We'll have to get going . . . as far away as we can. Otherwise we'll be caught, trapped! We'll have to go on, if not by car, then by train or bullock cart, or on foot, if need be! But go we must! Far, far away!'

The three of them shuddered in unison. 'Far away!' they repeated, over and over again. 'To the ends of the earth, if need be! Farther, maybe!'

I stared at them in astonishment. What a terrifying

creature was this *huliya*, to sniff us out here! And to fill them with such terror!

We sat on our divans as the moon sank slowly behind the trees and the room was filled with darkness. It was a long, long while later that the cawing of crows heralded the arrival of dawn.

Chapter 6

I think this was the first time in my life that I was happy to see the sun rise. Usually I had to be dragged out of bed, sometimes by the ankles. Of course, it could be because I didn't have to worry about brushing my teeth and washing my face or making my bed! However, the real reason for this happiness was that with the sunrise, all the worries and anxieties of the night vanished like dew.

Only one thought rankled in my mind. Did Shyamadas-kaka know magic? Where did the second necklace come from? That this wasn't the original necklace, I was absolutely one hundred per cent sure.

I looked out of the window. The sunlight glittered on the rain-washed trees and on the raindrops sprinkled on the enormous spider webs hanging in the bushes. There was a fresh newness in the air. I heard the lowing of the cow again. It sounded happy; perhaps it had caught something tasty!

I turned to look at the others. They were fast asleep

now, after the alarms of the night. *Why* were they so worried, I wondered. Something had made them so frightened that they were behaving quite out of character. Usually Thandidi couldn't bear the sight of Birinchi-da; as for Shyamadas-kaka and Birinchi-da, they never met without arguing over something. Yet they had spent an entire day in the same car and the entire night in one room, and never an angry word between them! What was *up*?

I opened all the windows to let in the sunshine and fresh air. The birds had begun their morning chorus; they sounded excited and happy, as though they, too, were infected by the freshness of the morning. The noise they made woke the other three. They sat up in bed, bleary-eyed and hunched up, looking as grumpy as grown-ups usually do when they haven't had their first cup of tea or read the newspaper.

Gradually, however, as they washed their faces and straightened their rumpled clothes, the brightness of the morning infected them and loosened their tongues. They seemed remarkably happy, I thought, considering the circumstances. In fact, they became positively garrulous!

Thandidi said happily, 'Well, Birinchi, I don't think you have any reason now to worry about ...'

Birinchi-da looked at me and hissed out of the side of his mouth, 'Hsshh—sshh—sshh!'

After a while he said with a happy laugh, 'Say, Shyamadas, maybe the fellow isn't dead yet!'

My uncle jumped nearly out of his skin and exclaimed, 'Shut up, idiot!'

I chuckled to myself. Now that it was daylight, they had all become very careless. I glanced out of the window, wondering where the old lady and old man I'd seen last night had got to, and saw a large crowd coming through the trees. Some of them looked rather familiar; also there seemed to be several . . .

'Policemen!' I exclaimed excitedly. 'Seven or eight of them. Now we don't have to worry about a thing!'

The words were scarcely out of my mouth when Thandidi and Shyamadas-kaka jumped up and rushed pell-mell into the bathroom. I gaped.

'Hey, where are you off to?' I said. 'Didn't I tell you the police are here? We're safe now. And . . . Oh, look, look! Here comes Shejo-dadu and Birinchi-da's Pishemoshai, his uncle!'

The next instant Birinchi-da had shot into the bathroom after them and slammed the door shut. I stood for a minute with my mouth hanging open, not knowing what to do. Then I, too, made a dive for the bathroom door and began to pound on the wooden panels.

'Let me in!' I yelled. 'Come on, let me in!' But there was no response.

Finally I gave up. Instead, I quickly slipped on my shoes and dived under the nearest divan. Whatever else happened, I wasn't going to leave my new shoes about for someone to nobble!

By then the entire party was inside the house, and coming up the creaky old wooden stairs. Then someone knocked on the door. I lay still. The knock came again, followed by someone saying in a hoarse voice, 'If you know what's best for you, you'll throw all your arms and ammunition outside the door. Then stand facing the door with your hands up!'

I lay mousy-quiet!

Then another equally hoarse voice said, 'Look here! Why resist the law and add to all your other crimes? Come out right away, and we'll make sure that you get a lenient sentence.'

Goodness!

Now it was Pishemoshai's turn. He seemed really angry. He came close to the door and began to yell all sorts of threats through the panels . . . most of which I didn't understand, and what I did isn't printable! Anyhow, the gist of his tirade was: 'Here, Birinchi, you stupid numskull! What d'you think of yourself, eh? D'you think you can do any (unprintable) thing you like and get away with it? If you know what's good for you, you . . . you (unprintable), then you'd better open the door pronto!'

Someone else spoke from a distance. 'Why don't you break down the door?'

Pishemoshai snarled, 'Oh yes, very clever! I break down the door and get my head blown to smithereens! No, thank you!'

Then I heard Shejo-dadu say, 'Anyhow, that's not our job. *You* are the official law-keepers. *You* break down the door. In any case, if you are blown up, your family will get a fat pension from the government, won't they? So why are you lot hanging back?'

The policemen were rather quiet at first. Perhaps the idea of being blown up didn't really appeal to them, pension or no pension! Then they got together, cleared their throats, stamped their boots on the wooden floor (sending up clouds of dust; I heard them coughing and choking) and thumped on the door with their batons. They must have been trying to flush us out.

At that moment the stairs creaked again. It was the old lady; I heard her panting as she almost ran upstairs to see what the row was all about. When she saw what the policemen were doing, she yelled with laughter.

'Oh my, my, my! What bravehearts! What supermen! You fools, can't you see, that door has no lock to it!'

Well, that was that! In one second, our brave police force, shoulder to shoulder, had thrust open the door and charged into the room, batons at the ready. Then they stopped and gaped in astonishment. The room was empty, not a soul to be seen! Where had so many people vanished?

From my position under the bed I could only see a forest of legs, among which those of the bearded man, the old woman and the oily youth were easily identifiable. They milled around rather haphazardly until they noticed the bathroom door. The fact that it was really and truly locked from within created something of a sensation, but by then the policemen had recovered their courage . . . probably because there were no desperate criminals in sight.

They ranged themselves in front of the bathroom door, cleared their throats, spat on their hands and jumped on the wooden panels in unison. The rusty hinges gave way with a melancholy creak and the door crashed into the bathroom, taking the law enforcers with it.

I was so excited and interested that I poked my head out from under the divan, to get a better view. Well, I thought, so that's that! It's all up with Thandidi and the rest of them. Serve them right, too! I had a sneaking feeling of sympathy for Thandidi, however. She really wasn't a bad sort.

But why this strange silence? There should have been a great deal of noise and screeching, especially on the part of Thandidi.

Forgetful of my own danger, I poked my head out further.

What I saw . . . or rather didn't see. . . sent my heart to the soles of my new shoes.

The bathroom was empty!

But . . . how was that possible? I had just seen three hefty adults run inside and shut the door. Where were they? The bathroom was small, and there was only this one door. There was a window, a skylight rather—but it was so small that even a cat couldn't have gone through it, let alone someone as plump as Shyamadas-kaka. As for Thandidi . . . my imagination boggled!

Then where were they?

Just then the others came back into the room . . . and spotted me at once! With yells of delight they flung themselves on me. One large fellow caught me by both ears and dragged me out from under the bed. I hung on to the leg of the divan for dear life, but to no avail!

Then they surrounded me and began such a hullabaloo as had to be heard to be believed. Each of them seized hold of me and tried to shake what they thought was the truth out of me. I began to get the nasty feeling that a little more of this and I'd come apart at the seams. Nobody would calm down long enough to listen to the whole story. The policemen yelled and stamped, and as for Shejo-dadu and Birinchi-da's Pishemoshai—the language they used was, to put it mildly, shocking for such old men!

'I tell you, I saw all three of them run into the bathroom and shut the door,' I kept on repeating as earnestly as I could. 'And now you say they aren't there! They *must* be there, you couldn't have searched properly. And even if they *aren't* in the bathroom, why pick on poor me? Look around the house; they're bound to be somewhere.'

By then Shejo-dadu was frothing in the mouth with rage. In fact, after finding me to be very small fry, he turned his wrath on poor Baba . . . and the things he said made my ears burn! Finally, realizing that I had nothing more to say, they handed me over to the policemen and went off to make a thorough search of the house once again.

Not that our brave law-enforcers were any better than Shejo-dadu. They hung around, trying to make me tell them what I had done to the other three. I began to get very annoyed myself. This was so unfair! Finally I burst out in Hindi (I always use Hindi when I'm angry, I don't know why!)

'Okay, okay, I've swallowed all three of 'em whole! *Now* are you satisfied? But just tell me, you nincompoops, *how* I managed to shut the bathroom door from the inside, when I was out here in the room! What about that, eh?'

Shejo-dadu and Pishemoshai had returned in time to hear my tirade. When I finished, the policemen looked sheepishly at each other, then went off to make another (fruitless) search. As they left the room, my own grand-uncle and Pishemoshai pointedly ignored me and strutted out with their noses in the air.

As if I cared!

Chapter 7

I sat quietly on the divan, swinging my legs and thoughtfully chewing a bit of gum. Suddenly one of the policemen began to shout loudly.

''ullo, 'ullo, 'ullo! 'ere's one of 'em!—*Got* 'im! . . . But where're the others, then?'

Wondering which of the three had been found, I went to the door, followed by the policeman who had been deputed to keep an eye on me. The other policemen were coming up the stairs, one of them triumphantly holding up by the shirt collar a thin, weedy, rather frightened-looking man. Who on earth was this?

They dropped the man on one of the divans and began to tie him up with gusto. Then they dusted their hands and stood back, surveying their prisoner with palpable pride.

The heroic captor threw out his chest and declared, ' 'e

was a-runnin' down the back stairs, 'e was. But I creeped up be'ind 'im, I did, an' spe-*rang* on 'im like a tiger!'

His colleagues applauded with a mixture of awe and envy. I looked at the poor captive. He sat there, panting and wheezing like an ancient and rundown steam engine. His eyes looked ready to pop out, he had lost a slipper during the fray, his moustache and beard stood on end, and his unshaven face was almost purple.

I exclaimed, 'Here, you've got the wrong person. I've never seen him in my life!'

The policemen rounded on me indignantly. 'Huh! That's what *you* say!' they snapped. 'This 'ere *indivijwal*, 'e's one o' your gang, i'n't he? An' you're a-tryin' to per-tect 'im from us!'

'Since I'm caught already,' I said, as patiently as I could, 'what's the use of protecting anyone else?'

But they just wouldn't listen! Finally one of them said, with an air of triumphant finality, ''e's got a dis-*guise* on, that's wha' it is! 'e's dis-*guised*, yes, a-wearin' o' beard an' mus-tache, an' you can't recognize 'im. That's what I say!'

Weird!

The thin fellow had been sitting quietly all this while, not even protesting when the men bound him hand and foot to the bedpost. Now he looked up, cleared his throat and began to say something but his captors wouldn't let him! One of them took off his turban and gagged him with that. Then they stood back with sighs of relief, dusting their hands on the seat of their pants and wiping their sweaty brows.

'Ouf! That was *dan*-gerous work, that was,' said one of them. 'Will you take a look on 'im? Ever seen such a ugly mug? Must be a des-prit wilain!'

'A 'ardened cri-mi-nal, that's what '*e* is,' added another.

'Yeh, you'd know it to look at 'im,' said the third.

'Well, that was thirsty work, an' me tongue's as dry as tinder! I need a bit o' smoke to wet me throat!' And the first policeman led the others out of the room, presumably to smoke their cigars or whatever.

As soon as the door shut behind them, I got up and went over to the prisoner. I wanted to have a good look at him, for so far I didn't have a clue as to his identity. He looked quite elderly . . . about fifty or so, or maybe fortyish. His arms and legs were very thin and there were tufts of hair in his ears. I felt very sorry for the poor fellow.

He must have sensed my sympathy for he wriggled his arms and legs and said, 'Egg—pgg—ggp!'

I gaped at him. What on earth did he mean?

He spoke again, pleadingly, 'Pgg—*gg*—*bgg*!'

This was most embarrassing, especially as the poor fellow was now purple in the face. I thought it wiser to call the policemen, but the minute I reached for the door handle, he thumped the floor with his heels and said angrily, '*Sss—ssh—ssh!*'

Anyway, the policemen returned just then and I drew a long breath of relief.

I sat down again and listened to the sounds of the great hunt going on in and around the house. Some of the policemen must have entered the kitchen to search there but they came out again in a hurry, and I heard the old woman's voice. She sounded far from pleased! A minute later there were footsteps flying up the stairs; then the unfortunate men tumbled into our room, bathed with sweat. Behind them came the old woman, muttering and waving a hot ladle at them.

Then she saw the prisoner and stared at him as though she had seen a ghost. The ladle dropped from her nerveless fingers and one of the policemen promptly picked it up and threw it outside the window. It's such ready wit and prompt action that get them results!

The old woman, however, ignored us all. She went closer to the divan where the prisoner was tied, still staring at him; her face was crimson and her hands shaking. The poor prisoner shrank back and tried to say something; he swallowed a bit of the gag and choked and coughed.

One of the policemen said warningly, 'Careful 'ow you goes, mum. This 'ere's a des-prit crim'nal, an' *bad* all through!'

The old woman said through clenched teeth, 'You don't have to tell *me* that, my child! Haven't I been married to him for years!' Then she faced the prisoner so suddenly, hands on hips, that he shrank as far back as he could. 'I'm glad this has happened,' she hissed at him. 'Serves you right! You deserved it!'

The prisoner said meekly, 'Llmm—*mmmlllmm!*'

The old woman ground her teeth at him and stomped off downstairs without bothering to look back. The policemen had been huddled on one side of the room, staring at her, open-mouthed. Now they emerged from their corner, wiping their brows and loosening their collars.

'Phew! What a dragon!' they gasped. 'Wouldn't like to 'ave to face that one ag'in!'

Then they stared at their prisoner rather despondently, wondering what to do with him. I suddenly realized something that I had forgotten all this while, thanks to all the excitements of the morning . . . I was famished! The sight of the ladle in the old woman's hand had made my stomach rumble uncomfortably. As always, when I was hungry, I felt depressed. I wondered where Thandidi, Shyamadas-kaka and Birinchi-da had got to, and I also wondered whether it would do any good asking the policemen for food. I decided it wouldn't!

Well, I always have an emergency stock about me, so I put my hand in my pocket. Immediately the policemen rose as one and fell on me with shouts. ' 'ey, none o' that, now, kid! Don' you go a-takin' out your knives an' guns, or we'll 'ave to blow your 'ead off with our sticks.'

I chuckled. 'If I *did* have any knives or guns or such-like,' I said, 'd'you think I wouldn't have used it on you before? No, this is chewing gum, my favourite food.'

The idiots refused to believe me! Probably they'd never even heard of chewing gum before, leave alone tasting it.

Finally I had to tear off bits of my precious hoard and give each of them a piece. Not that *that* helped much! They merely chewed their share thoughtfully for a minute or two and then swallowed it with one gulp. Then they sat there, looking dolefully at me.

Time passed with dismal slowness. The day was pretty far advanced, judging by the sun, which was shining down with unusual ferocity. It may have been eleven or twelve o'clock (on schooldays I finish my meal much, *much* earlier!) and the house was very quiet. Everyone must have gone out to search in the forest. I sat and wondered where Birinchi-da and the others could have gone. I had seen them run into the bathroom— and then they had vanished! Had the *huliya* got them, after all?

After a while, one of the policemen came up to me, patted me on my back and said jovially, 'Now, you is a fine young lad, you is! Like some sweeties, then?' I stared. He smiled, showing horrible, paan-stained teeth and went on, 'Come on, me lad. Jus' you up an' tell us where you've 'idden the bodies, an' we'll give you *ever* so many toys, we will. Kites . . . that big an' bright as you never did see! . . . *an'* balls *an'* spinnin' tops an' all. Now come on, be a sport, young fella. Tell us where the others are, an' we'll give you wot ye likes.'

The others came up to join him, and they surrounded me and tried to bribe me with all sorts of goodies, the crooks!

Suddenly the door was flung open with a bang, and the

bearded old man I had seen milking the ferocious cow swept into the room, flushed and panting. He fell on the unsuspecting policemen so suddenly and with such force that they were taken completely by surprise.

'You stupid *idiots*!' the bearded man said furiously, and he didn't look at all meek and suppressed. 'Numskulls! Can't catch the *real* thieves, and all you do is catch our Babu! *And* truss him up like a chicken, too! Just you wait and see . . . each of you'll have to serve a twenty-year jail sentence for this! *I'll* see to it! Imprisoning our Babu, indeed. If you haul him off to prison, who's going to pay our salary, tell me that? You lot?'

The unfortunate policemen had had a bad morning from the start. Now they cringed back as the storm of words broke over them. The old man didn't wait for them but began untying the prisoner himself.

I said, 'You'd better take the gag out of his mouth.'

But there wasn't any gag; the prisoner had swallowed it! The policemen were highly indignant. 'What d'you mean, swallowed it?' they exclaimed.

One of them added, 'It 'ad me laundry list, it did. An' wot am I to tell me ol' 'ooman now?'

By then the prisoner had recouped his energy and, it seems, his temper. He glared at the policemen and snapped, 'What d'you mean, swallowed it! It practically went down my throat!' Then he grinned, licked his lips to clear it of a few remaining threads, and added, 'Not that it tasted bad! Nice and spicy and chutney-ish!'

The very sight of him licking his lips made me realize just how hungry I was!

In the distance I heard Shejo-dadu and Pishemoshai; they were talking to the police inspector and they sounded thoroughly disgruntled. Obviously my three companions hadn't been located as yet. Seriously though, where *were* they? Had something tracked them down and . . .

The police inspector was saying, 'He may be a kid, and he may look small, but there's no doubt that he's at the bottom of this affair. Otherwise, how could the others come up with such a plot?'

Pishemoshai immediately chimed in, 'Exactly! *Just* what I was saying! My Birinchi was never like this. It's all because of that fiend in boy-shape. My poor nephew believed in him, followed him, and met a nasty end in the forest.'

Shejo-dadu wasn't going to allow Pishemoshai to have the upper hand, whether he secretly agreed with him or not. 'Don't talk of your nephew as though he's an angel without wings,' he said sharply. 'Birinchi's just as bad, if you ask me. Look at the way he wheedled my poor sister-in-law into . . .'

The inspector interrupted hastily. 'Look, if you don't mind my saying so, sirs, these family matters are nowhere near as important as the matter of the necklace. Whether Birinchi or Shyamadas lives or dies won't shake the earth, but if I don't find the zamindar-babu's wife's necklace, my boss'll eat me alive. And what about me losing the chance of a promotion, eh? What about that, tell me!'

Chapter 8

They trailed despondently into the room and sank down on the nearest divan. Then, looking at me out of the corners of their eyes yet speaking as though I wasn't even there, they began to talk all at once.

'Look at him, sitting there as innocent as you please, looking as though butter wouldn't melt in his mouth! Yet there isn't a worse criminal anywhere in the world. Doing away with three grown-ups overnight! Just imagine!'

Birinchi-da's Pishemoshai sighed and said, 'You know what has hurt me the most? The fact that that idiot Birinchi vanished wearing my best silk kurta and . . .'

Shejo-dadu sat up. 'Shhh! We mustn't speak ill of the dead,' he said piously. 'What's happened has happened! It's all water under the bridge, time gone is gone forever, and so on and so forth. Now, the most important thing is: the inspector should cross-question this innocent-looking criminal and get all the information out of him.'

All this while, the rest of us in the room had been listening to them, open-mouthed. Now all of us tried to get our own versions heard first . . . and the noise we made was indescribable! Finally, the inspector came up to me, placed his hands on my shoulders and said in a fatherly way, 'Come now, son. Tell us what you've done with the bodies . . . and with everything else. You know about the necklace, of that I am sure. Just return that and we'll let you off. Nobody will harm a hair on your head, I promise. Give me the necklace, there's a good fellow.'

What was I to do? After all, I'm just a small, innocent little boy ... something that these hulking adults refused to believe! I thought, well, there's nothing for it but to have a shot at finding them. So I drew a deep breath and went to the bathroom door.

The others crowded round me eagerly as I stepped across the shattered panels and looked around the tiny bathroom with eagle eyes. If there was a clue, I thought, then I would find it. I hadn't been mistaken, though. There was something decidedly queer about the disappearance of my three companions. I mean, the bathroom wasn't very big, and there was only one door and one tiny barred window, set fairly high up. Nobody could get through that.

The others were clustered around the door, breathing heavily down each other's necks and staring at me with a mixture of awe and respect. Even the old woman had left her cooking and come upstairs to watch me in action. I heard them whispering to each other, 'Shh! Not a sound! He's going to take out the necklace, now, and find whatever else all the others have lost!'

The old lady stared at me, mouth and eyes round 'O's of surprise.

I suddenly noticed something small and glittery, lying on the floor behind the heavy iron bucket. As I stooped and picked it up, the others surged forward into the room.

I stared at the small golden ring lying on the palm of my hand.

Shejo-dadu gave a sudden shout. 'It's my sister-in-law's ring!' He rounded on me so suddenly that I jumped nearly out of my skin. 'I knew it! I knew he was behind it all, and yet he refuses to admit his crime, the villain!—You'll be crushed under the mountain of your sins, you miserable liar! There won't be place for you even in Hell!'

The police inspector turned menacingly towards me. In sudden panic, I ran out into the middle of the bathroom—and got a worse shock! The ground opened up beneath my feet, suddenly and sickeningly, and I found myself falling through black, interminable space!

Loud shouts echoed in my ears from somewhere far above me. Then—silence.

I don't know how long the fall lasted. It seemed hours and hours must have passed . . . although in reality it couldn't have taken more than a few minutes. I thought of *Alice in Wonderland*, and wondered whether I, too, would come out at the other side of the earth. I thought of all the naughty things I had done since infancy; I repented of all my past misdeeds, most of which I had forgotten, some of which I hadn't even committed.

Then, suddenly, with an almighty thump, I landed on solid ground.

Actually I landed on a pile of hay, on a most tender part of my anatomy, which is why I didn't get as badly hurt as might have been expected. Still, I sat quietly for a while, eyes shut, breathing heavily, until I was convinced that I was still alive and one hundred per cent myself.

Then I opened my eyes very, very slowly and looked around. The first thing that struck me as surprising was that it wasn't really dark, although I was sitting at the bottom of a dry well, its stone walls festooned with centuries-old cobwebs. The mouth of a tunnel yawned open before me; it smelt musty and old but a faint light was reflected on the walls.

In that slight glimmer I saw, lying on the straw beside me, the second necklace. I picked it up with shaking hands. The blue stone in the centre glowed with rainbow radiance. I sat there and stared at it, wondering where it had come from and whom it really belonged to. Was this the necklace stolen from the wife of the zamindar-babu? Then what about the other necklace? Who did that belong to? I knew that this was the second one, because no one but myself would be able to take out the first necklace. And I had my doubts about that, too!

I slipped the necklace into my pocket, feeling rather upset. That the other three had come down the same way, there was no doubt. The necklace itself proved it. But where had they gone after that? Something terrible must have happened to them, otherwise they certainly wouldn't have left the necklace behind.

I imagined my three companions falling down the well and landing on the pile of hay, one on top of the other. They must have been terrified out of their wits! But the very fact that they weren't there proved that they must have found an escape route . . . and if *they* had, so would I! Looking round carefully, I was sure that the tunnel was a way out; the faint light seemed to show that.

I wondered who had made the tunnel, and what use it had been put to. The house above was obviously ancient, and goodness only knows how many other tunnels there were. Undoubtedly they had been used for all sorts of nefarious dealings by the makers—perhaps to transport stolen goods, maybe to imprison enemies . . .

I felt a cold shiver run up my spine.

I got up and began to walk cautiously along the tunnel. It must be very, very old, I thought. In ancient times people must have hauled huge chests full of treasure and gold coins along this way. Ooohhh, if only I could lay my hands on even one such chest, I wouldn't have to waste my time doing useless lessons in school!

Surprisingly, the tunnel was not as dark as I had expected, considering it was so far underground. I could just make out empty shelves, covered with inches thick dust, and iron rings fastened to the wall. Enemies of the smugglers must have been hung from those rings—and suppose a skeleton or two still hung there!

My heart began to beat uncomfortably fast, and I began to walk faster.

Of course, I was safer down here than up in the house with Shejo-dadu and the rest of them. But . . . what if something fell on my head? I heard the flutter of invisible wings, things brushed against my face and strange smells assailed my nostrils. Bats, I thought, and began to walk faster than ever until I was practically running.

The tunnel had changed somewhat. It sloped downwards and the walls and floor were now made of earth. There was an unpleasant dampness in the air, and occasionally a drop or two of some liquid fell on my head. Whether they were white or red, I didn't stop to see!

Thandidi, Birinchi-da and Shyamadas-kaka had come down this way just a short while ago. I pictured them walking in single file, shivering in fright, huddling together as they walked. Of course, they must have passed on safely because I didn't find any bodies lying around.

The thought had barely crossed my mind when I stumbled over something and fell on my knees. Suddenly the tunnel seemed to grow very dark and queer sounds kept echoing in my ears. I gingerly touched the *Thing* I had fallen over. It was soft and very still; I tried to make out whether it was breathing or not. But suppose it was not?

And then . . . !

I sat up suddenly, every sense alert. A soft padding sound came to my ears, followed by heavy, rather snuffly breathing. Was that . . . was that one of my companions? Had I found them at last?

But the sounds were different . . . strange! I stood up slowly, screwing up my eyes, trying to figure out who . . . or *what* . . . was there. At first I couldn't see a thing. Then two tiny red pinpricks of light appeared in the darkness behind me, followed by the snuffling and a peculiar smell that *seemed* familiar, but . . .

But I didn't stop to analyse what it was. My life was too precious to me. I took to my heels and fled down the dark, damp, earth-smelling tunnel!

Chapter 9

The tunnel sloped downwards fairly steeply now as I stumbled along as fast as I could, feeling along the dank walls, trying to keep upright. Then it turned a sharp bend and ended in a kind of hallway with a huge wooden door. I fell up against it and, to my relief, it swung open. In a trice I was through it and had slammed it shut, pulling the heavy wooden bolt across it.

I leaned against the door, panting and wheezing, my heart thudding like a piston. But I was safe, at least for the time being.

As in the tunnel, there was a faint glow in this place, too. I could dimly make out the shapes of huge objects . . . barrels and boxes, they seemed. And on the nearest box was a candle in a stand, with a matchbox beside it. I lit the candle as quickly as my shaking hands would allow, then held it up over my head.

In the flickering light I saw that I had found Aladdin's cave!

Never have I seen so many precious and beautiful objects hoarded in one place. Magnificent carpets hung on the walls, some of them reaching from ceiling to floor. Great piles of plates, dishes, jugs, pots and pans, vases . . . some made of copper, some of bell-metal, some even of silver. There were richly carved tables and chairs, the tables piled with boxes, harmoniums, gramophones. Wonderful paintings hung on the walls between the carpets.

I cautiously opened one or two boxes. They were stuffed to the brim with incredible treasures. One box was filled with expensive silk saris, another had watches of every size, shape and make that I could think of, a third had silver bowls and dishes, another had fountain pens. I even found one that had . . . believe it or not! . . . gold jewellery.

I wandered about in a kind of daze. I didn't know what to do with all these treasures. Shyamadas-kaka had nearly fainted with joy and excitement at finding one pearl necklace, and I had treasures uncounted! Plus one pearl necklace.

I took out the necklace from my pocket and put it on the box of jewellery, wondering how to take all my treasures home. Absent-mindedly I pressed one of the harmonium keys; it was in perfect condition, the sound filling the closed room and echoing round and round, making me jump. I chuckled; just a few days ago Birinchi-da had nearly eaten me alive for dropping water on his harmonium. And now I had four brand-new and one not-so-new instrument.

But I was hungry. And when you are hungry, as any fool knows, you can't enjoy anything. I hadn't had anything to eat or drink since last night and my tummy was letting me know all about it, in no uncertain terms.

I looked around, but not with any hope of finding anything edible. The paintings on the wall seemed to be moving and shifting in the flickering candlelight. There was one of an old lady with her hands folded and eyes shut in prayer, obviously giving thanks to someone for the dish of fried fish placed before her on the table, while a huge cat tried desperately to get at the goodies. There was another painting of the same cat running off with an enormous lobster in its mouth.

I hadn't eaten anything since last night!

I couldn't bear it any more. Anything was better than being so hungry, even being caught by the *huliya*. I ran to the door and pulled it open with force. Immediately, as if he had been waiting for me to do just that, the bearded man pushed past me and entered the room. Then he turned and stared me up and down, hands on hips.

I glared back defiantly. 'Do what you like to me. Kill me, slit my throat, shoot me, string me up . . . I don't care! I'm hungry . . . more hungry than I've ever been in my life!'

The old man said, 'Why didn't you tell me that before?'

Then he opened a box, took out a towel or two and revealed tins of sardines, packets of biscuits, a bottle of orange squash, plates, glasses and a tin opener. It was food for the gods!

The old man had seen the pearl necklace. He fairly beamed as he put it away in the box of jewellery, then went to shut and lock the door. Then we perched ourselves on the nearest chest and had a superb feast. After we had finished every scrap of food, the old man wiped his mouth on a filthy hanky and offered it to me. I didn't need any such thing; I always use either my shorts or my head.

The old man looked at me with twinkling eyes. 'You're small,' he said, 'but really clever. Will you join my gang? Maybe one day you'll become the chief.'

'Who's the chief now?'

'Er ... myself!'

'Huh, you're old. You won't be chief for very long ... May I have some more orange squash, please?'

Just at that moment someone began to push the door from outside. We looked at each other as whoever it was thumped the door again. Just then the candle flickered and went out. We hastily and noiselessly hid the remnants of our feast behind one of the boxes. Then we sat silently, side by side, and awaited the events.

After a while I whispered to the old man, 'Suppose they break down the door?'

The old man snorted. 'Break down this door, indeed! They're scared of their own pet cow, d'you know that? They're incapable of breaking down *any* door!'

'But ... suppose the police are doing the pushing?'

'That's why I'm not opening the door!'

I was right! It *was* the police.

They began to shout all sorts of dire threats through the panels. 'Open up at once, or we'll set the house on fire!—We'll lock the door from outside!—We'll set bogies on you!' etc.

I felt a wee bit nervous, but the old man sat tight. He didn't seem in the least nervous . . . just like the chief of a gang . . . until we heard the old lady's voice.

'You'd better come out,' she roared, 'and sooner than at once! Otherwise I'm going to let all the cats out of all the bags, and so I warn you! If everyone comes to know about the goat affair that took place the year before last, well, don't blame *me*! That's all!'

The old man jumped to his feet and began to pace nervously about the room, despite the darkness. 'Never trust women, my boy,' he told me. 'You never know what they're about! Turncoat! Blackleg!'

The old woman's voice came again. 'Remember that day, the January before last, when you got up at the crack of dawn to . . .'

The old man couldn't bear it any longer. 'Here, shut up, you!' he yelled. 'I'm warning you—!'

He was so furious, he pulled open the door and stepped right out. I had no option but to follow him and try to hide myself behind him. Then I peered out from under his arm. To my surprise, there was no one there except the old lady with a small lantern in one hand and her inevitable ladle in the other.

The old man was thoroughly annoyed at the old woman's ruse. 'Think yourself clever, huh? Where are they?'

'Where are who?'

'The police, of course!'

'How should I know? Gone back to their duties, I hope.

I'm not their keeper! In any case, when I came downstairs, they had broken into your room, and they were lying there with their booted feet up on your nice, clean bed, smoking your cigarettes and reading your diary. Very funny they found it, too. All sorts of spelling mistakes, and that!'

'What spelling mistakes?' yelled the old man angrily. 'Anyway, so what if there were spelling mistakes? Why'd you let 'em get away with it? Aren't I your elder brother? And why are you down here, instead of keeping an eye on them?'

'Oh yes! I stay up there, and you get away with everything, leaving us paupers.' Suddenly she spied my legs. 'Aha, got hold of an apprentice, have you? Well, I don't care. All I want to know is . . . have you seen my boy?'

The old man was just going to answer, when we all heard the tread of many feet coming our way down a passage. Brother and sister looked at each other, white-faced. Then they slipped noiselessly into the room, pulling me in with them, and shut and locked the door.

We stood just by the door, as quiet as mice, our hearts thudding so loudly that we were sure it would be heard by the others. A large group of people had really come up the passage to the door.

Chapter 10

There was no way of knowing whether the people were friends or foes. However, one thing was certain—the two in the room were much, much nicer than any of the others. The old woman was such a wonderful cook!

By then the people outside had begun to hammer on the panels, accompanied by such shouts and yells as had to be heard to be believed! But it was practically impossible to break down that huge, heavy wooden door.

Suddenly we heard a snorting, grunting sound, coming from somewhere inside the room. All three of us jumped nearly out of our skins! What on earth was that? The old woman promptly hid behind her brother. Finding nowhere else to hide, I quickly opened the cover of the nearest chest and tried to climb inside. But there was something . . . or someone . . . inside. I jumped back with a screech of fright.

A dead body!

The old man and the woman nearly fainted with shock, too, especially when the body began to sit up slowly. I sprang back even further. The body was now staring at me without blinking. As the old man lit another candle, my breath slowed down and I felt a wave of relief sweep over me.

It was Birinchi-da!

Thank goodness! Another minute, and I'd have died of heart failure!

Birinchi-da clambered out of the box, stretched and yawned like a cat, brushed down his clothes, smoothed his hair; then he chuckled suddenly. Most probably at the snorts and grunts that were still audible . . . and which I suddenly recognized!

I went up to two of the biggest boxes and opened their covers. In one of them Thandidi lay in a dead faint; in the other was Shyamadas-kaka, curled up like a puppy and fast asleep. We had heard his snores echoing through the room. However, the minute Birinchi-da leaned over and poked him in the ribs, my uncle sat up and demanded, still with his eyes shut, 'Got the necklace?'

The old woman gave a snort of annoyance. 'What do you want with the necklace?' she demanded. 'It doesn't belong to you.'

'It doesn't belong to you, either,' retorted Shyamadas-kaka, opening his eyes so that he could glare at her.

I said, 'What about Shejo-dadu, Birinchi-da's Pishemoshai and all the policemen? They're all hanging about outside!'

Everyone sat down suddenly, looking rather pale.

Birinchi-da asked anxiously, 'I say, Goopy, is Pishemoshai alone?'

I said, 'Didn't I tell you just now that Shejo-dadu and the police inspector and about a dozen policemen were with him?'

'No. I mean to say . . . er . . . the thing is, were they all . . . what d'you call 'em . . . *men*?'

The trials and tribulations of the past hours must have driven poor old Birinchi-da mad.

The old woman said, 'Anyhow, where's the necklace? We'll have to decide what to do with it.'

The old man looked annoyed. 'Well, the necklace doesn't belong to you, so why are you so bothered about it?' he exclaimed. Then he perched himself on the very box in which he had kept the necklace.

I felt a little anxious about Thandidi. 'What about rousing Thandidi?' I asked.

'Oh, let her be!' snapped Shyamadas-kaka. 'She's better this way! The moment she wakes she'll drive us wild with her constant blah-blah-blah!'

The words were hardly out of her mouth when Thandidi sat up and glared at Shyamadas-kaka. 'You bad, wicked boy!' she snapped. 'Blah-blah, is it? D'you want me to tell everyone of your misdeeds?'

Shyamadas-kaka retorted, 'Hah, be careful you don't get involved in them as well!'

Thandidi clambered out of her chest and in one minute several warring factions had formed in the room—Thandidi and Birinchi-da one side, Shyamadas-kaka on the second and the old woman and her brother the third. Poor me! As usual, I was stuck in the middle.

Birinchi-da asked me again, rather urgently, 'Goopy, are you sure Pishemoshai was all alone? I mean, was there a priest with him, or a young woman in a red sari?'

'No, but there are any number of policemen.'

The old woman had been rooting all over the room. Now she came back and faced her brother. 'Where's the necklace? Tell me, where is it?'

The old man said, 'It's not your necklace.'

'Well, and why shouldn't it be mine?' retorted the old woman. 'Why should it belong to the zamindar's wife and not to me?' She sat down on one of the boxes and went on, almost to herself, 'How many, many times have I seen it around her plump, fair neck . . . just like a row of gleaming pigeon's eggs with an enormous diamond glowing in the centre! Look, just tell me one thing: she's rich and fair; otherwise, in what way am I worse than her?'

Her brother gave a short laugh. 'You and your eyesight! The stone in the centre isn't a diamond, it's a blue sapphire.'

'Don't teach me, brother,' snapped the old woman. 'I've seen it too many times to make a mistake. Every year, during Pujas, I've seen her wearing it to the temple. And each time I've pictured myself coming regally down the steps of the temple, with a vermilion dot on my forehead, wearing a beautiful silk sari with a broad red border and that necklace round my throat . . . and everyone staring at me and turning green with envy!'

The old man glared at her. 'Now, just wait a minute,' he snapped irritably. 'You just can't say anything you like and get away with it. I know for a fact that the stone is blue . . . a blue sapphire . . . and if you don't believe me, I'll prove it to you.'

He jumped off the box, opened it and pulled out the necklace. Then he held it up. 'See?' he exclaimed triumphantly.

In the dimly lit room, the pearls glowed like small moons, and the stone in the centre caught the flickering light of the candle and flashed blue fire. The old man dangled the jewel in front of his sister. She stared at it as if hypnotized.

For a long, long moment there was silence. Then the old woman said in a half-whisper, 'No no, *this* is not the necklace! I know it isn't! I haven't lain awake night after night, dreaming of this necklace. You've got the wrong one!'

Just at that moment, something creaked and rattled in the loft, high up near the ceiling. All of us looked up uneasily. The flickering light of the candle did not reach the corners and shadows hung about the ceiling like huge bats. We huddled together, feeling positively scared.

The creaking came again, louder this time. Then the loft gave way with a tremendous crackle and a large, rather ungainly bundle fell to the ground with a resounding thump, then turned over and sat up. I stared, astonished. It was the skinny man the police had caught by mistake . . . the old man's Babu!

He gave himself a shake and stood up, rather unsteadily. We saw that he was actually laughing. 'My goodness, I've been hanging on to the rafters for so long, I must have gained a good six inches or so! My muscles feel all stretched and rubber band-ish! Thank goodness I fell off the loft because I was laughing so much!'

The old woman asked sourly, 'What was so funny, eh?'

'You, m'dear, you!' The skinny man snorted and choked as he tried to control his merriment. 'Imagine you in a silk sari and pearl necklaces. I nearly fell sick with laughing.' And he began to giggle again uncontrollably.

I looked rather anxiously at the old woman; surely she would burst with rage. But she was staring at the necklace as though hypnotized. When she did speak, her voice sounded sleepy and faraway.

'They lie under the rolling waves, the oysters, on the golden sand of the sea bed. They open and shut, gulping in sea water. Sometimes a grain of sand gets in and that irritates the oyster. So it gives out a milky white substance that it wraps round and round the grain of sand. The sand gets covered and the oyster loves the smooth, silky feel of it. Then one day a diver comes down with a glass mask over his face and a long air tube to help him breathe in water. And he picks up the oyster, many such oysters, and the pearls are taken out and made into necklaces for the likes of the zamindar-babu's wife. But this necklace is not the one she wears!'

By then the yells and thumps outside had subsided; in fact, it was very quiet. Except for me, everyone seemed very relieved. No one thought of taking the necklace away from the old woman. Birinchi-da began to explain what had happened to them.

'I knew we were in for a bad time when we fell through that infernal hole in the floor! Oohh, the darkness and the fright! Not to mention Thandidi landing right on my tummy like a sack of potatoes. What a weight! It's a wonder my tummy and its appendages are in proper order.' Here Thandidi snorted indignantly as Birinchi-da continued, 'Anyhow, we walked through the tunnel for miles and miles. It was horrible! To top it all, we heard stealthy footsteps following us down the tunnel. We saw its eyes burning in the darkness. Some slavering monster, no doubt, or the first cousin of the Hound of the Baskervilles!'

The old man gave a snort of laughter. 'Hound of the Baskervilles, my foot!' he exclaimed. 'And no slavering monster, either. It was only my little babesie-wabesie, my precious Tippy's lovely baby!'

'Who on earth is Tippy?'

'My sweet little cow, of course!'

We fell silent, staring at each other, somewhat abashed. Then Shyamadas-kaka, who had been wandering all over the room, said more to change the subject than anything else, 'Where on earth have all these priceless things come from?'

No one answered. Really, I've never seen so many beautiful things in one place at one time. I was just about to repeat my uncle's question, when we were startled nearly out of our wits by loud yells from outside.

'Help, help! Save me, save me from the monster! Oh my goodness me! Help!'

What on earth—?

The old woman felt sorry for whoever it was; in spite of Thandidi's anxious warnings, she pulled open the heavy door. Immediately a total stranger fell rather than entered the room. He was plump and fair, with long curly hair and soft white hands. He was dressed somewhat foppishly in a fine dhoti and richly embroidered kurta plastered to his body by perspiration, and a glittering diamond ring. But for all his fine clothes, he was a sight to behold! His long hair stood out around his head in wild disarray, his face was as white as paper and his eyes were starting from his head in terror.

He sank down on the nearest box, shaking all over like a leaf. We stood around him in a silent circle, wondering who he was and what news he had for us.

It took him quite a while to regain his breath. He sat there, wheezing and gasping; then, with a long shuddering breath, he drew out a large white handkerchief and wiped his brow with trembling hands.

'Thank goodness for small mercies!' he managed to gasp after a while. 'If you hadn't opened the door just when you did, Didi, that monster of a cow would surely have eaten me up whole! Just imagine, being swallowed by a cow! And yet I've done such lavish puja every year for the last thirty years, even sent a pair of goats to the temple during Kali Puja! And *this* is the result!'

The old woman turned to her brother, looking thoroughly annoyed. 'You've let your precious Tippy loose again, have you? How many, many times have I told you to keep her tied up? Now she's been wandering all over the place, and if her calf drinks up all the milk, how am I to manage tomorrow's tea, may I know? Just like a man to be so careless!'

The fat, fair gentleman looked at her and wiped his brows again. 'Let us survive until tomorrow morning,' he gasped. 'Then you can think about making tea!'

Chapter 11

He turned his head to squint up at the old woman . . . and saw the necklace in her hand.

To say that he was startled is putting it mildly! He jumped as if he had been attacked by a ghost and began to wheeze and tremble all over again.

'Goodness! Where did you find this?' he demanded.

Then he leaned forward and stared at the necklace again. 'Oh no, it's not the same one! But it looks alike!'

Everyone promptly fell on him and bombarded him with questions. 'What necklace? Whose necklace? What d'you mean different?' And so on and so forth.

Birinchi-da even went so far as to add, 'I can help you find the real necklace, you know!'

I had to laugh. Birinchi-da . . . help!

The gentleman said, 'I am the zamindar-babu whose wife's necklace was stolen. You see, the situation is this: the necklace was insured for a tidy sum and if it was stolen, all that lovely lolly would come into my pocket. But how *could* anyone get anywhere near it, with the wife practically sitting on it day and night! Anyhow, finally someone did manage to . . . er . . . steal it, but what a hullabaloo after that! Really, that wife of mine has no sense. There was no need for such a tremendous fuss and botheration, but no! She had to go and call in the police!'

Sitting in that underground room, the zamindar-babu went on aggrievedly, 'I told her time and again . . . explained to her ... that there really was no need for the police to get involved. I mean to say, why get them into the house? It wouldn't do anyone any good, not us, not the country! In any case, I told her, I couldn't do any running around, I had terrible tummy cramps. But would she listen? No sir! She sent that idiot brother of hers and got an entire police battalion into the house!'

We stood listening sympathetically as he continued pouring out his woes. 'Of course, the inevitable happened after that, as anyone would expect. Sniffing around everywhere and popping uncomfortable questions at everyone ... investigation and interrogation, *they* call it! ... and driving everyone to the brink. To top it all, my genius of a cook gave notice and departed bag and baggage. I don't know whether he will return, alas! You know, when I saw that necklace, I nearly had a heart attack. Thought that the wife's necklace had been found and so goodbye to all that cash! Thank goodness, though, it's not her necklace.'

'Then how was the necklace stolen?' I asked eagerly, unable to keep quiet any longer.

'That's the problem!' exclaimed the zamindar-babu. 'I mean to say, if I knew *how* it was stolen, I'd know *who* did it! But that's neither here nor there. The crux of the matter is that the necklace has vanished from the strongbox and my wife's behaving as though the world has come to an end. I really didn't expect her to react in this way. That's why I had to leave the house.'

Birinchi-da edged closer to the gentleman and said ingratiatingly, 'We might be able to help you find it, sir.'

Instead of being pleased with the offer, the zamindar-babu snapped irritably, 'Oh, for goodness' sake, don't try to be such a do-gooder!'

The old lady, her husband and brother had been listening in open-mouthed silence all this while. The zamindar-babu suddenly rounded on them, making them jump nearly out of their skins.

'Tell me, do any of you happen to know the whereabouts of a skinny chap with long, oily hair and golden rings in his ears?'

We gaped at the zamindar-babu in astonishment; as for the other three, they turned as white as a collection of sheeted ghosts. The zamindar-babu looked at their pale faces in surprise.

'So, you *do* know him?'

The old woman spoke first, in a hoarse whisper, through barely parted lips, 'Why? What do want with him?'

'My dear lady, he's got me into such hot water! If only I had him before me for a minute, I'd show him!'

The thin man had been crouching behind a large chest all this while. Now he came forward and said angrily, 'Oh, you'd show him, would you? We'll see who shows whom! One slap from him and you'd go flying through the window, and all your fancy airs and graces with you!'

'Ah ha! So you *do* know him, then!' the zamindar-babu spoke triumphantly.

The thin man looked sheepishly at him. 'No, no, I'm telling you, we don't know him, haven't seen him, haven't even heard of him. And he certainly doesn't live here.'

The old lady began to sniffle. 'He hasn't done you any harm. All this is just a plot to ensnare a poor, innocent boy. No, we don't know him, and he hasn't been here since yesterday evening.' She gave a heart-rending sob. 'Ooohhh, don't you have any feelings, or are your hearts made of stone?'

The zamindar-babu looked terribly embarrassed. 'Now, now, dear lady, don't you misunderstand me,' he said hastily, in conciliatory tones. 'Please don't cry. See, I had thought that he was a nice guy and one whom I could trust. But thanks to him, I'm neck-deep in hot water with the prospect of either facing the police or my wife . . . and I don't know which is worse!'

Then he took a good look at the necklace and went on, 'Of course, this necklace *is* very like the other one, of that there can be no doubt! But it's not the right one. I wouldn't make a mistake! I remember my grandmother wearing it and my mother staring at it, green with envy. Then my mother wore it and my wife would stare enviously. Now Mother is old and the wife wears it. It's insured for a lakh of rupees, do you know, but the thieves nowadays are such a worthless lot, they can't even open a simple safe and steal it! Huh, you can't depend on them any more.'

He sat down on a box and went on, 'Just imagine: generations after generations of mothers-in-law, going back to the time of the Flood, wearing that same necklace and making generations of daughters-in-law turn green with envy. It doesn't bear thinking about! But now that's all over . . . my wife's the last man in! Hah! Now, if only somebody could help me meet that young man, I'd give him ten rupees on the spot.'

The bearded man instantly stretched out his hands. 'Where's the ten rupees, then?' he said with a grin. 'Let's have a look at it.'

The old lady and the thin man instantly fell on him, grabbed him by the beard and began to yell breathlessly, 'No no, don't you listen to him, sir. He's a terrible liar, he is! No one knows anything about that boy, sir.'

The bearded man sat up and glared at them. 'Ho! Liar, am I?' he said, carefully beginning to free his beard from their grasp. 'I'll show you who's a liar! Who had the bowlful of cream yesterday? I'm your elder brother, I work all day, and yet do I get the biggest piece of fish? No sir! They're scared to death of their own cow, yet I never get one glass of the creamy milk she gives. All right, show me that ten rupees you were talking about.'

The zamindar-babu coughed in an embarrassed manner. 'Er . . . the fact of the matter is, I do have ten rupees, really, but . . . er . . . it's in my purse, at home! In the rush and all that, I sort of left it behind.'

The old man glared at him. 'Just as I thought!' he exclaimed wrathfully. 'Trying to worm out our secrets with false promises. Okay, I won't say a word until I see that cash.

Then I'll think about it. There are so many things that I forget, but I remember later, and . . . *ouch*!'

The old lady had pinched him at a particularly tender spot and he fell silent.

At that moment the loft above our heads creaked and cracked in a most alarming manner. We stared upwards and the thin man said anxiously, 'Oh, don't bother about that. It's just that I had been sitting there for so long that the beams have become rather loose and are swaying and creaking. There's nothing there, I tell you! . . . Why won't you listen to me and look away? There—is—no one—there! Look, there's a pillow that fell with me. Oh, for goodness' sake!'

We ignored him and continued staring upwards. The wooden beams of that ancient loft had been tied together with ropes. Now the ropes snapped in two and hung down, swaying slightly. The beams parted company and fell to the floor, bringing with it a shower of old pillows, sheets, rugs, mattresses, one red slipper . . . and the long-haired, lungi-clad youth wearing the other red slipper!

He scrambled to his feet, dusted himself down and turned to face the zamindar-babu. 'Okay, so here I am! Where's the ten rupees, then?'

We gaped at him. The old lady said, in a hoarse whisper, 'Run for your life, son. These people are only out to get you into trouble.'

Her son ignored the warning. Inching closer to the zamindar-babu, he said again, 'Well, where's the money, then? I've shown myself to you, haven't I?'

All this while, Thandidi had sat in absolute and, for her, unusual silence. Now she suddenly found her voice. Turning to the old lady, she asked, 'Who on earth is that oily youth, the one with the earrings?'

The old lady scowled ferociously. 'That, madam, is my son,' she snapped. 'And that thin gentleman is my husband. Does that bother you? And do you have any more questions to ask?'

Thandidi was quite equal to the occasion. 'Oh yes, my child, that I do,' she retorted coolly. 'A great many questions, in fact. What on earth are all of you up to, tell me that? Wandering around in the middle of the night with hooded lanterns. Secret trapdoors in the bathroom. Underground tunnels and hidden chambers full of boxes, all filled to the brim with stolen goods, I expect.'

There was a sudden silence in the room after she finished, a silence so intense that you could have heard a pin drop. After a long while the old lady said, 'Why, what's that to you? And if you don't like it, go ahead, call the police and hand us over. Go on. The house is infested with them, as it is, and your relatives are hand in glove with the police, too!'

Shyamadas-kaka and Birinchi-da rounded on Thandidi. 'Why do you have to poke your nose into the affairs of others?' they chorused irritably. 'Why can't you leave well alone? If the police come in, will Shejo-dadu and Pishemoshai be far behind? Then you'll be in real hot water and drag us in after you.'

I had discovered the last piece of chewing gum in my pocket . . . rather hairy, but still edible. I prised it off the cloth, rubbed of the lint and was just about to pop it into my mouth when there was another round of thunderous knocking on the door.

A hoarse voice said, 'Open up, open up! It's the police here. Open the door, or we'll blow it down, we really will!'

There was dead silence in the room. Everyone scattered like frightened chickens, looking for a hiding place. The oily youth and his father scrambled up the wall like lizards and vanished into the depths of another loft. The rest of us dived into boxes or behind hangings and harmoniums.

The hoarse voice came again—perhaps it was the inspector. 'Open up! Whoever obeys, will get five rupees.'

The next moment we heard a weird grunting sound, followed by squeals of 'Oh my goodness me! The monster! . . . It's got me, it's got me! . . . Here, Haran, you idiot, shoot it, shoot it! . . . Ooohhh, eeek! Help, help, it's bitten me . . . shoot, shoot it!'

The bearded man shot over to the door, flung it open and called anxiously, 'Here Tippy, Tippy baby! Here, Tippsie-wippsie! . . . Cooey-cooey-cooey!'

The grunting sound came again and then the ferocious-looking cow I had seen before appeared in the doorway and glared around with red eyes. Behind her stood a calf that looked just as carnivorous as her. The bearded fellow stroked them lovingly.

'My poor babies! My poor darlings! Did those nasty men frighten you? Did they hurt you, then? Poor mites, you're looking as pale as ghosts!'

The entire police contingent had vanished. Tippy and her baby pushed their way into the room and showed that they were hungry by beginning to chew on the bearded man's trousers. He tried, ineffectually, to skip out of their way.

'Hey, Tippy, stop that! Stop it, babesie-wabesie, that's my trousers! Here, what's got into you two? . . . Okay, okay, come with me and I'll find something for you to eat.'

The bearded man found some ropes and tied mother and child up; then he led them off, presumably to find prey for the famished beasts. The rest of us heaved collective sighs of relief, emerged from our hiding places, wiped our brows and looked at each other somewhat sheepishly. I scraped the chewing gum off my fingers and popped it into my mouth.

'Now to relax!' I thought.

I should have known better!

There was a dry cough behind us, and the inspector and his entire contingent stepped into the room, followed by Shejo-dadu and Birinchi-da's Pishemoshai.

I jumped and swallowed the final bit of my precious chewing gum without even tasting it.

Dash it!

Chapter 12

The room seemed suddenly full of people. There were about a dozen of them facing us—and we had tried so hard to stay out of their clutches since the previous day! Ironic, I call it!

Anyway, the rest of us forgot our own disagreements and stood facing our foes, scared but resolute. In the front row stood the zamindar-babu, then Thandidi and Shyamadas-kaka. Then came Birinchi-da, the old lady and her long-haired son, behind them the thin man and finally, a little to the rear and hidden . . . I hoped . . . from the general view, myself.

The inspector took out a small black book and a red pencil, remarking as he did so, 'I really don't know where to start, or with whom. I don't think I've ever seen so many criminals gathered together in one place, at least not since the infamous Bhubondanga gang was caught!'

The man standing beside him, a real yes-man, if ever there was one, smirked and said, 'Exactly! You're perfectly right, sir. Just you wait and see, sir—for this glorious deed your name will be splashed in every newspaper in the country. You might even win some kind of an award or something, sir, you never can tell! Maybe a Third Prize of some sort!'

Someone else added, 'Begin with that small boy, sir. He's only a boy and if you frighten him a bit, he'll spill all the beans.'

At that, Birinchi-da's Pishemoshai exclaimed, 'Don't you

be fooled by that cherubic appearance! Don't be misled into thinking that here's a sweet, innocent child. He's the leader of the gang, I tell you, the arch-villain!'

Shejo-dadu, however, wasn't going to let one of his family be maligned, whatever might be his personal opinion. 'You needn't talk about arch-villains, sir,' he snapped. 'Your Birinchi is just as bad, if not worse.'

The inspector seemed rather put out by this exchange of pleasantries. He gaped from one to another, looking so confused that finally I took pity on him and stepped forward to introduce myself.

'My name is Goopy Chakrabarty,' I said. 'I'm eleven years old and study in Class VII. I'm four-and-a-half foot tall and I weigh about . . .'

The inspector interrupted, 'That's enough, kid. Children should be seen and not heard.'

Ungrateful, I call it!

The inspector then turned to Thandidi and asked, 'What's your name and address, madam?'

Thandidi promptly covered her head with her sari, turned her back to the inspector and exclaimed, 'Goodness me!'

Shyamadas-kaka said, 'Her name's Nistarini Devi. Address—43 Harishankar Lane, Calcutta.'

The inspector scribbled the information down and asked again, 'Reason for coming here?'

Birinchi-da leaned forward and said in an audible whisper, 'Shall I tell them about the Gaya trip?'

The yes-man promptly leaped forward. 'No, no, no, no!

We call that "harassment of the witness" and that's strictly illegal . . . not allowed . . . no, sir!'

Thandidi, however, took the hint and said cheerfully, 'Oh yes! Of course! We were on our way to Gaya, and our car broke down in the middle of the jungle, so we took shelter here. And if there's any crime in taking shelter for the night, my boy, I have yet to hear of it!'

The inspector was just about to make a note of that in his book when Shejo-dadu said, with a snort of contempt, 'Gaya, my foot! You can't fool me, any of you! I know what you were up to, Sister-in-law. You were getting away with my mother's jewellery, just in case I presented them to my Gurudev . . . I won't utter his sacred name before this pack of sinners! But I won't let you. Let me remind you that only a third of those jewels belong to you, the rest of it belongs to me and to Goopy's father. Oh, poor Gurudev! How you must be suffering without your golden mug!'

The inspector stopped writing and stared at Shejo-dadu. Then he edged closer and asked confidentially, 'Would you care to repeat that, sir? That bit about your Gurudev taking someone's golden mug, or something. I didn't quite catch it. Would you kindly repeat your statement, sir?'

I couldn't help giggling at that. Shejo-dadu did not answer. He flopped down on a box and began to wipe his forehead. The inspector waited for a minute or two, then turned to the old woman.

'Now, my dear lady, tell me your name, please, and something about your career, as well.'

'The name's Swabhavsundari Dasi,' came the sharp answer, 'but I won't tell you anything about my curry. That's *my* specialty, that is!'

The yes-man said irritably, 'Nobody wants to know anything about your curry, madam. Just tell us, simply and clearly, what work you do.'

'What don't I do!' replied the old lady. 'Mainly cooking, of course. And a host of other things. . . . But my son doesn't know the zamindar-babu, whatever anyone else may say to the contrary.'

She clutched her son's hand, but he released himself and said glumly, 'I didn't know him all these years, but I do now . . . and very well, too!' He turned on the unfortunate zamindar-babu and said, 'Now then! Cough up my hundred rupees . . . and pronto!'

The zamindar-babu patted him on the shoulder and said ingratiatingly, 'Now, now, dear boy! Don't get agitated. I promised you a hundred rupees and I will give it to you sooner or later.'

The inspector shook his head in a confused manner, shut his notebook and said wearily to the yes-man, 'I can't make out head or tail of what is going on. You try and unravel the whole affair, Shambhu.'

Shambhu didn't have to be told twice! He grabbed Shyamadas-kaka and Birinchi-da, pulled them out of line and opened fire on them. 'You two are the ringleaders in this affair! Now, no use trying to deny that, it's written all over your faces. There's no doubt about it . . . anyone can see that you're crooks and con men! I wouldn't be at all surprised if it was found that you're at the bottom of that smuggling racket that's just come to light in England! Now then, if you know what's good for you, just you open up and confess everything.'

Poor Shyamadas-kaka and Birinchi-da! They gulped, bit their tongues several times, interrupted each other at the most crucial points, much to the wrath of Shambhu, and after several contradictions and U-turns, finally managed to stutter out a barely coherent account of the happenings of the past two days.

When they had finally meandered to an uncomfortable silence, the inspector glared at them and said, 'I see!'

Then he turned to Birinchi-da's Pishemoshai and said, 'Now then, sir, what do *you* have to say about all this?'

Pishemoshai said glumly, 'What can I say? I had arranged a very suitable marriage for that ungrateful rascal with my best friend's daughter. Everything was ready for the big day, clothes and accessories had been bought, the priest had been fixed . . . and you know what the rascal did? Just vanished! Vanished without a trace!' Suddenly he rounded on Birinchi-da. 'Why did you run away, you idiot? Tell me why!'

Birinchi-da went scarlet. 'Er . . . well, you see . . . Shyamadas said the girl was a bad-tempered dragon and breathed fire and smoke at the slightest excuse.'

'Oh, I see! So "Shyamadas said", is it? It's always the same. "Shyamadas said this" and "Shyamadas said that".'

Pishemoshai glared at Birinchi-da. 'And do you know what your precious Shyamadas has done? Why he had to run away from home?'

'Here, hold it . . .' began Shyamadas-kaka, but Birinchi-da's Pishemoshai swept on inexorably:

'Yes, your precious Shyamadas . . . he walloped his own uncle—his Mama—and then vanished. And why did he beat up his poor old uncle? Because all that gentleman had said was, "Rave as much as you like over Kanai Chatterjee or Goshtho Pal, there's really one footballer worth the name, and that is . . ." That's all he said!' Pishemoshai glared at Shyamadas-kaka, then went on, 'He didn't even get a chance to mention the name, when Shyamadas flattened him, and then skedaddled! So now you know what kind of a person he is! Shyamadas—hah!'

The old lady had been listening to all this in open-mouthed wonder. Now she uttered a little squeal and exclaimed, 'Oh my goodness me! Just imagine—a thief, a runaway and a murderer! And I'm scared to ask about that fiendish little thing! To think I let them spend the night in my house! It's a miracle we're alive to tell the tale!'

The inspector smiled. 'As you say, madam!' he said dryly. 'Now, how about giving me a list of all the stolen goods so neatly stored here?'

The old woman looked astounded. 'Stolen goods?' she gasped, indignantly. 'What stolen good? These are all the gifts I received at my wedding, from my parents as well as my in-laws. I've been looking after them for these twenty-

five years or more, making sure no harm comes to them.'
And she stroked one of the harmoniums affectionately.

At that moment, the bearded man reappeared, having
fed his fierce pets adequately. The inspector looked at him
for a moment, then took out his purse.

'How many months since you were last paid?' he asked.

The old man's face lit up. 'Six months, sir, six whole
months!' he said excitedly. 'Would you believe it, sir? And I
her own elder brother, too. They make me do all their work
for them, are afraid of their own cows, yet they won't give
me a penny! They owe me for six months, sir; that's ... let's
see now ... sixteen into six ... that is, sixty-four.'

The inspector thrust a ten-rupee note into his hand and
said, 'Yes, well, keep this for the time being. Now, who on
earth steals these things? And who sells them again?'

The bearded man said, with palpable pride, 'Oh, we have
our team, sir. Hand-picked, everyone of 'em, and trained
by me. I have about a score of them, now, in my pay. And
d'you know which one is the cleverest? That long-haired
bo ... mmmm!'

He was cut short by the old lady and her husband, who
pounced on him and stifled him with their hands. The old
lady said, in breathless agitation, 'Don't listen to him, sir.
He's a terrible liar, he is. Really!'

The inspector had been noting everything down in his
small black book. Now he shut it with a snap and said, 'Well,
that clears up everything . . . except the matter of the
necklace.' He looked around at everyone with a smile and

said, 'Don't worry about anything. I'll stop you from being hung or even imprisoned. But that necklace has me worried, you know. Without that, how will I get my raise?'

Everyone shook their heads sympathetically. The inspector rounded on the zamindar-babu so suddenly that that gentleman gave a guilty start.

'Now, see here, sir,' said the inspector. 'Is this fair? Is it just? I mean to say, you're a rich man but that doesn't mean you can stand in the way of our rise in the world! I've been very patient with you all this time but now I think I'm going to lose my temper. Are you sure this isn't your necklace?'

The zamindar-babu shook his head in a rather helpless manner and swallowed once or twice. The inspector glared at him in annoyance.

'Why isn't it your necklace? What's wrong with it, eh?'

'Er, it isn't the one my wife wore,' began the zamindar-babu, looking about him in a hunted way. He gulped and added, 'That long-haired youth . . .' He stopped abruptly.

'Go on, go on! Why are you stopping? "That long-haired youth" . . . what?'

Before the gulping zamindar-babu could say anything, the oily-locked youth pushed forward.

'Shall I tell you everything, sir?' he said, with a great show of paan-stained teeth.

'Oh dear! Now, see here, m'boy,' said the zamindar-babu, in great agitation. 'Just keep your mouth shut and I will, I really will give you your hundred rupees. Oh dear, what a mess!'

The inspector looked very annoyed. 'Look here, just stop all that nonsense and come clean, please,' he growled. 'I want to hear the whole story . . . and the whole truth!'

'Can't I leave out a few bits and pieces?' said the zamindar-babu pleadingly. 'Just one or two . . .'

'No!'

The zamindar-babu winced. 'But . . . but . . . what about the stuff the wife has said about . . . er . . . about the police?' he bleated.

'Oh, very well, you can leave out those bits, if you like.' The inspector looked thoroughly disgruntled. 'Now, get going, please. And remember, I want the whole truth!'

The zamindar-babu plumped down on a low box and wiped his face again. 'Okay, as you say,' he said in a resigned voice. 'That necklace is a family heirloom. It costs a pretty penny, I can tell you—a lakh of rupees. And that's the amount it was insured for. If it was lost or stolen, I would get one lakh rupees in my pocket.' The zamindar-babu sighed heavily. 'There seemed no chance of such an eventuality, though, for the wife guarded it with her life. She never let it out of her sight! All day it hung about her neck and she would sleep with it under her pillow.

'And then one day, that necklace vanished! Into thin air, my dear sir, just imagine that. There wasn't a soul around, the door was locked from inside . . . yet in the morning my wife found—no necklace!'

The zamindar-babu drew a deep breath and continued, 'Well, it was gone . . . but if you'd only seen the fuss my wife created! Turned everything upside down, she did! And as for the insurance company officers, I've never seen such a suspicious lot!' The zamindar-babu shook his head. 'Just you think of it, sir. Year after year I've paid a fat premium and yet when it comes to paying up, what do they do but bombard me with questions: how was it stolen, where is it now, are you sure it was stolen, what proof of theft do you have? And so on and on and on! Finally, in desperation I showed them this young man's footprints . . .'

Everyone stared. 'Where on earth did his footprints come from?'

The zamindar-babu looked around at all of us in a rather hunted manner. Then, turning to the inspector, he said appealingly, 'Do I *have* to tell you everything? If the wife heard of it, she'll . . .' He broke off, shuddering.

'Oh, for goodness' sake! Who on earth is going to go and blab to your wife?' The inspector snorted. 'What happened next?'

'Well, okay, if you're sure she won't hear any of this!' The zamindar-babu seemed partially relieved. 'Well, I told the young man . . . You don't have to do a thing; just stand underneath the window and I'll throw down the necklace to you. Then you vanish! Later, you can hand the necklace over to me at an appointed place, the level crossing, say . . . and I'll hand over a hundred rupees, and that will be that!'

The oily youth sniffed and the zamindar-babu said in aggrieved tones, 'He was in no danger. I told him so! Tell me, sir,' to the inspector, 'did he have any call for this show of temper?'

'No, no, of course not.'

'Is that all you have to say?' For the first time the zamindar-babu showed a spurt of temper. 'That young fellow, whom I trusted so highly, just vanished with the necklace. He wasn't anywhere to be found, not near the level crossing, nowhere. To top it all, thanks to the wife, the whole place was simply swarming with policemen, all of them intent on following me closer than my own shadow! And I haven't had time to draw breath since that day.' He turned to the long-haired youth with a return of his pleading manner. 'Give back the necklace now, there's a good fellow! I don't need the money; I just want to return the necklace to the Big Boss of my family and be done with all this fuss and botheration!'

The oily youth immediately pointed to Shyamadas-kaka. 'Don't ask me, ask him.' Everyone stared and he continued, 'I believed you and went off with the necklace. But how was I to know that you'd set the police after me!' The zamindar-babu spluttered indignantly. 'I did go to the level crossing but it was thick with policemen intent on capturing anyone they thought looked like a thief. What was I to do? I had to save my skin, so I slipped the necklace into *his* pocket and shot off home. Ask him! As for me, I've had enough of stealing. I'm going to go straight, so help me god! I'm going back to school, so long as I'm put in the same class as Montu and Potla!'

At which declaration, the old lady and the thin gentleman

rose as one and fell on his neck with tears of joy and kissed and cuddled him right in front of all of us. That hulking fellow! Oh, the shame of it!

Chapter 13

In the meantime, everyone had rounded on Shyamadas-kaka.

He promptly turned all his pockets inside out, raised his hands in the air and said, 'I don't have it, I promise! You can search me, if you like. I'm even willing to take off my pyjamas. I don't have it, I gave it to that rascal Goopy first thing. Here Goopy, hand it over at once, if you know what's good for you. What's the point of hanging on to someone else's thing, especially as it's caused so much trouble!'

I took off my shirt and my shorts, turned them both inside out and proved to all there present that not only did I *not* have the necklace, I didn't have several buttons, either!

The inspector stared. 'Then where did the original necklace go? And where did this second one come from?' he asked in astonishment.

At this the oily youth blushed all colours of the rainbow, scratched his head and mumbled, 'Er . . . well . . . I sort of took it from Dad's General Stores.'

The thin man had put up with a great deal throughout the day. This was obviously the last straw! He rounded on his son with a stinging slap and exclaimed, 'From my shop!

No wonder it looked so familiar! Why did you steal it, you rascal?'

The oily youth gulped and said meekly, 'Er . . . won't it be better if I told you sort of . . . privately, like? Look, Daddy, don't blow your top, please. I did it for both of us; you know, we'd both be the gainer.'

The inspector opened his well-thumbed notebook again and said in long-suffering accents, 'A little slower, please, or I won't be able to get it all down.'

The long-haired fellow said somewhat mutinously, 'I'll get into all sorts of trouble if I tell, won't I?'

'Don't worry! In any case, be a man, my lad! What's a little trouble here and there for you?'

'Okay, but if you put me in jail, I won't be able to play in the league matches in Chandannagar. All right, I'll tell, but you'll have to give me ten rupees first.'

'Give it to him, Shambhu,' said the inspector, in resigned tones.

The oily youth fairly beamed. 'You see, sir, I thought I'd hand this fake necklace over to the zamindar-babu, sell the original one and live happily ever after.'

'Oh, the treachery!' The zamindar-babu shuddered.

The meek old gentleman fired up at once. 'Libel! Don't you dare malign my son's character! After all, he has a reputation to live up to, doesn't he? In any case, *you* can't talk! Not having the courage to steal your own wife's necklace and getting someone else to do your dirty work for you!'

Birinchi-da, Shyamadas-kaka and I spoke together. 'What happened next?'

The long-haired youth glared at us. 'As if you don't know what happened next!' he snapped. 'You vanished with the real necklace and I came home with the fake one and found that you had taken shelter with us for the night. Well, I thought, that's that and the bird is safely in the coop, and all that sort of thing. All in vain! The necklace was nowhere to be found although we searched you with a fine-tooth comb. To top it all, I left the fake necklace in someone's pocket by mistake. Now, out with it. Where is the necklace?'

The inspector looked at me. 'You look such a baby! Who would think that you're such a crook! Give me the necklace.'

Shejo-dadu added his two bits. 'I knew it would all end this way! I told your father, don't give him that wristwatch, but who listens to an old man. Give back the necklace and I'll . . . I'll give you some chewing gum.'

Birinchi-da's Pishemoshai said, 'Really, I've never seen or heard of a family with so many crooks and con men all together!'

Everyone fell on me, talking all at once. 'Give up the necklace at once!'—'Give back the necklace, boy, please!'—'Wot's the 'arm hin 'anding it back, m'lad?'

And so on and on and on!

Finally the zamindar-babu came up to me and patted me on the back and said pleadingly, 'Just think of my situation, boy! Please give back the necklace or my life won't be worth living, I tell you! I'll give you a dozen chewing gums, I really will, if you give me the necklace.'

What was I to do? I am only a poor little boy, after all!

I said to the bearded man, 'Chief, lead the way out of here.'

The bearded man saluted and started off, all of us falling into line behind him. Someone picked up the stub of the candle and within seconds the secret room vanished into the darkness behind us.

The bearded man led us along a narrow, twisting passage that ended in a short flight of uneven steps that led into the old woman's cavernous, fragrant kitchen. Outside, in the courtyard, Tippy and her baby were chained to metal posts; they stamped their forefeet and licked their lips when they saw us.

The old man paused. 'Oh my poor sweeties! My babesies! Are oo's hungry, then?'

We pushed him on and passed the beasts with a good deal of space to spare.

Outside, it was high noon. The rain had stopped and the sun blazed down from a cloudless sky. High overhead a kite circled round and round, like a tiny dot against the blue sky. Everything looked sparklingly fresh . . . and unchanged, which I found most surprising! So much had happened through the night that I felt the house and its surroundings would be totally different.

But the forest looked the same as we took a narrow but well-defined trail through the towering trees, followed by a line almost a quarter of a mile long. Most of them, I was told, were representatives of the zamindar-babu's insurance company. He grumbled about them constantly . . . but under his breath!

Then I heard Birinchi-da say meekly to his Pishemoshai, 'Er . . . about that wedding . . .'

'Don't bother!' snapped that gentleman. 'I've arranged the marriage with my sister's son, instead. Botta is a diamond of the first water, a million times better than you.'

This seemed to give Shyamadas-kaka courage enough to ask, 'About that fellow I . . . er . . . beat up . . . er . . .'

This time Birinchi-da's Pishemoshai spoke almost genially. 'Oh, that fellow won't die so easily! I owe him money, you know. If you had to kill him, why do it so half-heartedly?'

Shejo-dadu looked at Thandidi with a faint smile. 'Well Sister-in-law, seems that all your partners in crime are throwing in the towel!' he remarked. 'What have you to say to that?'

Thandidi didn't utter a word. Instead, from the folds of her shawl she took out her huge red pouch. Without stopping in her stride, she extracted two or three things, then threw the pouch at Shejo-dadu's feet. As he bent to pick it up, Thandidi said sourly, 'Goopy, tell your father to demand his fifty per cent share.'

Shejo-dadu didn't reply to this, for by then we had reached the spot where we had abandoned Birinchi-da's much-tried car. It still stood under the tree, slightly lopsided and rather battered-looking. Everyone surrounded it in a breathless circle with myself in the middle, the cynosure of all eyes.

I said, 'Does anyone have anything sharp and pointy? Thandidi, what about one of your knitting needles?'

'Where do you think I'll get a knitting needle in the middle of this jungle!' growled Thandidi.

Females! Honestly! They never seem to have anything useful or important with them when you need it most!

Anyway, I tried again. 'What about a ruler or something?' There was an uneasy silence. I said, 'Well, without the right tools, I can't help you, you know.'

Finally Shyamadas-kaka went to the car and pulled out a long, stiff wire from the glove compartment. I almost snatched it from him and poked it down through the gap beside the front left-hand window. It took several breathless minutes of wiggling and poking and manoeuvring, but finally I managed it.

I pulled out the real pearl necklace!

Last evening, while rolling up the window, I had dropped the necklace in the gap!

I rubbed the necklace on my shorts and held it up to the light. The diamond in the centre glowed with an inner fire. The zamindar-babu almost ran forward and snatched it from my hand.

'Yes, here is it! My lost treasure! *This* has driven me from hearth and home and given me so many sleepless nights! Oh, let me hold it close to my heart once again!'

The insurance company fellows pressed forward,

elbowing us out of the way. They bent over the necklace and suddenly one of them exclaimed, 'Hullo, hullo! What have we here?' His eyes narrowed. 'This one's a fake as well!'

A storm of protests broke over him. 'What d'you mean . . . fake?'—'This is the real one, all right!'—'Are you blind, or what?'

But the insurance company officer was not to be put off. 'It's my job to know the real from the fake,' he said. 'I get three hundred rupees a month for doing just that. If that necklace is real, then I'll . . .'

The zamindar-babu rushed forward at this point and covered the man's mouth with a plump, fair hand.

'Hssshhh! Please! Don't even *dream* of saying such things!' he whimpered. 'Okay, okay, I admit I had to sell it last year. I had such a run of bad luck that . . . And if my wife couldn't make out that this was a twenty-five rupees fake, then why should *you* be bothered?'

The officer sighed. 'Well, I'm not really bothered,' he admitted. 'But I do have my report to write, you know.'

'Write your report. Write out a passport, if you like!' snapped the zamindar-babu. 'As long as word of this doesn't reach my wife! . . . Why don't you let it go, old fellow, and I'll give everyone a . . . a fiver. Come now, that's a promise.'

The bearded man snorted. 'You don't even have *one* five-rupee note, and you're promising to pay the entire lot,' he said scornfully.

The police inspector had been a silent spectator all this

while. Now he sighed and said, 'Well, I understand everything more or less ... rather less than more! All except that bit about the underground passages.'

The old woman gave him a hopeful look. 'If you promise to let everyone off without a charge, I'll tell you all about that, too,' she said. 'We've decided, my old man and myself, that we'll retire and our little boy will go to school.' She simpered.

The inspector laughed. 'You don't have a thing to worry about, madam, if you hand over all the goods stored in the passages,' he said. 'After all, there's no case against you or your family. *My* job was to find the zamindar-babu's wife's stolen necklace ... and that is done! Her ladyship will reward me for that. As for you, if any case against you comes up, we'll deal with it at the time.'

'And what of my baby boy?' The old woman sniffled.

'Baby boy!' Shambhu, who was still hanging around the inspector, looked indignant. 'He's neck-deep in bribery and corruption, and you call him a baby.'

It was the oily youth's turn to fire up. 'I haven't received a penny from anyone,' he said crossly. 'What do you mean bribes?'

The zamindar-babu looked round rather helplessly, and the bearded man came to his rescue. 'He really doesn't have a penny,' he said.

The old woman sighed. 'Oh, all right, I'll tell you as much as I know,' she said resignedly. 'Years ago, the house used to belong to an Englishman who made a fortune through making illegal arrack. Rumour had it that he used rotten shoes to distil the alcohol. Finally, when he had made more money than even he could dream of, he went back to England and became a famous doctor or a Lord, or something.'

'And the house?'

'Oh, my grandfather bought it off him dirt cheap.' The old woman looked pleased and proud. 'My father inherited it; then, when I got married, he gave it as my dowry. When we discovered that the tunnels were still in mint condition . . . well, we couldn't waste them, now, could we? That's the only mistake we've made . . . if it can be called a mistake!'

The inspector shut his notebook with a snap, tucked his pen in his pocket and drew a deep breath. Then, with the necklace in hand, he waved to the zamindar-babu to follow him and strode off down the path. The old woman and her skinny husband followed, pleading and arguing.

The rest of the crowd evaporated like a lump of camphor left in the open. One minute they were all there, the next . . . only us four were left, staring blankly at each other.

A thought struck me and I drew a deep, regretful breath. 'No one . . . but no one . . . gives anything away for free, do they?' I said. 'Certainly not a packet of chewing gum!'

Shyamadas-kaka and Birinchi-da spoke as one. 'No one, no one! Never!' Shyamadas-kaka added, 'Haven't I told you, life's just a load of garbage in a dustbin! . . . Now, let's make a move. We've got to find a motor mechanic's shop before we can get back home.'

Home!

Suddenly I felt a great balloon of happiness welling up inside me. Yes, we must get home. Boggai must have searched for me all of yesterday and last night!

Translator's Note

The quintessential 'children's author' Lila Majumdar proved that stories can effortlessly transcend the barriers of age and space.

Although she wrote in Bengali, her fluidity and universality made her works beloved even among those who are non-Bengali, because she never believed that communication can be marred by man-made barriers of language and culture. A happy spirit and an innocent, searching mind is common to every race, culture and country . . . and these very things are the golden threads that link all her stories, weaving a magical pattern of enchantment that never fail to touch all who read them.

That life isn't mundane and exciting changes can happen in a very short space of time and change people's lives forever is apparent in 'The Burmese Box', which takes place over just a day and a half. The past flows into the present, linked by the mysterious box reputed to be filled with fabulous treasures. Dreams dictate actions that take place in the real world; Podi-pishi is alive and well in the young boy's dreams, issuing orders as to what he should do after finding the box. And when the box is found, the lives of the characters are never the same again.

In 'Goopy's Secret Diary', life changes for another young boy, and again over a short period of time, no more than a couple of exciting days. Lila Majumdar obviously didn't believe in long drawn out actions, just as no child appreciates long-term planning! The protagonist in the story lives through a very exciting day and night, during which he experiences a gamut of emotions and comes in contact with a host of people, all with their own quirks and curious traits of character.

It was these quirks of human nature that the author found so fascinating. She always felt that it was these oddities that kept one young, even when the inevitable physical process of ageing took its toll on us. It was these qualities that were reflected in her child protagonists, and which she wanted everyone to nurture and cherish till the last day of one's life. It was the waywardness of human nature that kept one alive and kicking, she used to say.

Many readers have wondered at her predilection for using boys as her protagonists. There are very few stories where girls come to the fore. The reason for that is, as a tomboyish young girl, she envied the freedom a boy had over the greater restrictions imposed on girls of that time. That is why she rarely used girls to embody her vision of the magical world in which all of us live. It was only towards the end of her life, interacting with her great-granddaughters and the girls of the twenty-first century, that she began to change her mind about girls in general!

Translating her thoughts from the parent Bengali into English, a different language and a different thought process altogether, wasn't easy. In fact, I prefer to call it a 'transcription' rather than a direct 'translation', for that is an impossibility in terms! But I have tried to retain the flavour of her stories, the happy spirit that can always see the silver lining to every cloud and anticipate the sunshine after the showers. Lila Majumdar loved life, enjoyed every aspect of it and tried, through her writings, to convince people that life was not just for living, but for living happily.

That joyous celebration of life was what she passed on to me, the love of one's surroundings, the sky above, the earth below, the world all around. And for that I shall be eternally indebted to my darling Didibhai, my grandmother.

August 2010   Srilata Banerjee

Born in Kolkata, Srilata Banerjee grew up all over the country, in cities like Jamshedpur, Lucknow, Patna and Madras, among others. From her earliest days, she was always interested in writing and drawing. This interest began at a very young age, with making up stories to tell her grandparents, including her maternal grandmother Lila Majumdar. Later, several short stories were published in Sandesh, *the Bengali magazine. Her short story 'Bondhu' was published by Ananda Publishers in their collection of ghost stories,* Ek Baksho Bhoot. *She has taught in schools like Miranda Hall and Morning Glory, and was principal of the Alipore branch of Harvard House.*

With her children now grown up and ample free time on her hands, she has several stories for children, both in English and Bengali, in the pipeline. The translations of Lila Majumdar's works are her tribute to her mentor and dearly beloved grandmother.

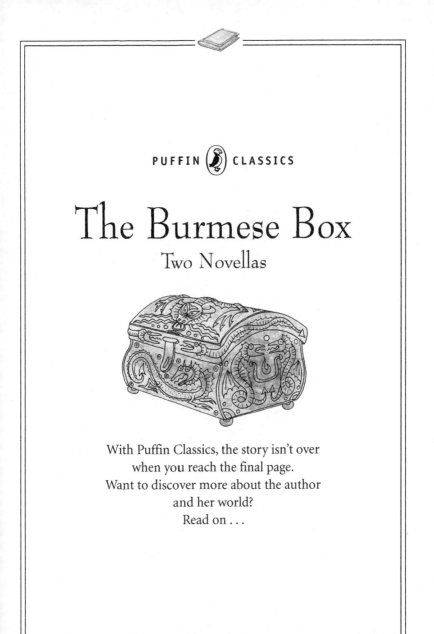

PUFFIN CLASSICS

The Burmese Box
Two Novellas

With Puffin Classics, the story isn't over
when you reach the final page.
Want to discover more about the author
and her world?
Read on . . .

CONTENTS

BORN: 26 February1908 in Kolkata.

PARENTS: Surama Devi and Pramada Ranjan Ray

FAMILY: Her father was the younger brother of Upendrakishore Roychoudhuri, who was the father of Sukumar Ray (noted Bengali author and poet, who created works like *Abol Tabol*, published in English as *Wordygurdyboom!)* and the grandfather of Satyajit Ray (noted film-maker and creator of Feluda and Professor Shonku).

EDUCATION: Early education in Shillong (now, capital of Meghalaya). Took Matriculation (Class X) exams in Calcutta and stood second among girls (in 1924). Studied English Literature for graduation and Masters. Stood first in Calcutta University for both exams.

INITIAL CAREER: Worked as a teacher in Darjeeling, Santiniketan (started by Rabindranath Tagore, who invited her to teach there) and then in Calcutta. She also worked for All India Radio.

CREATIVE CAREER: First story published when she was a teenager, in *Sandesh* (a popular children's magazine, founded by her uncle Upendrakishore and then edited by her cousin, Sukumar).

First book *Baidyanather Bori* (Baidyanath's Pill) was published in 1939. Became famous with the publication of her second book *Din Dupure* (Midday). Both were compilations of humorous short stories, usually written from the perspective of children and captured everyday life. A prolific writer, she wrote many poems, short stories and novellas and is one of the best writers for children in India. She also co-edited the magazine *Sandesh* for a long time, along with Satyajit Ray, her nephew, and Nalini Das, her niece.

Apart from writing for children, she has written autobiographies, cookbooks and household tips—all of which have been very popular.

AWARDS: She has won many awards for her works, including the Sangeet Natak Akademi Award in 1963 for a comic musical drama called *Bok Badh Pala* (Death of the Demon Bok). Her autobiography *Aar Kono Khaney* (Somewhere Else) won the Rabindra Puroshkar in 1968, and *Holdey Pakhir Palok* (The Yellow Bird) received the President's award for best in children's literature in 1960.

DEATH: 5 April 2007 in Kolkata.

RELATIONSHIPS IN BENGALI

The two stories have a large number of characters, who are related to the narrators, and all of them are called by their relation.

Relationships in Indian languages are very specifically described. Father's elder and younger brother or Mother's brother are all called Uncle in English but have different names in Indian languages. For example, it is *Tau*, *Chacha* and *Mama* in Hindi.

In Bengali, the relationships are further classified by the seniority in the family.

For example, Boro is the Eldest. Chhoto is the Youngest. Mejo means the Middle. In the case of four siblings, the third sibling is the Shejo.

Some of the relationships mentioned in the stories are:

Podi-pishi	Pishi = Father's sister. Podi is the name of the lady, who was the 'pishi' of the generation before the narrator. So, strictly speaking, she should have been his grandmother and not aunt.
Pishemoshai	Pishi or Father's sister's husband
Panchu-mama	Mama = Mother's brother. His name was Panchu.
Shyamadas-Kaka	Kaka = Father's younger brother; called Chacha in Hindi. Shyamadas is the name of the gentleman.
Didima	Didima = Mother's mother or Nani.
Nimai Khuro	Khuro = another name for Kaka or Chacha, Father's younger brother. The gentleman's name was Nimai.

RELATIONSHIPS IN BENGALI

Khuri	Paternal Uncle's wife or Kaki/Chachi
Mejdimoni	Mejdi = Mejo Di = The second elder sister. 'Moni' (meaning jewel) added to the name is an affectionate term.
Shejodadamoshai	Dadamoshai = Mother's uncle. Shejo indicates that he is the third uncle in seniority, that is, Nana or Grandfather's third brother.
Chhoto-Kaka	Chhoto = youngest. This means Father's youngest brother.
Thandidi	Thandidi = Father's mother. Also called Thakuma.

In your mother tongue, do you have similar classifications for relationships or seniority? Can you say what the above relationships would be called in your language?

Diarists

Goopy had a secret diary and the story unfolds from his point of view, as if he is writing his diary. What do you think of his entries? Were they written like diary entries?

Actually, the diary style of writing novels has been used for several important and well-known books of all times. Here is a list of some very interesting diary writers.

ADRIAN MOLE

This British teenager first appeared in the book *The Secret Diary of Adrian Mole aged 13³/₄* and soon became very popular. The books—written by Sue Townsend—are about growing up in England, Adrian's attempts to become a writer and his girlfriend, Pandora. It started with Adrian being a teenager and the series continued to his adulthood and eventually, middle age.

PROFESSOR SHONKU

The genius inventor, created by Satyajit Ray, maintains a regular diary and almost all his adventures are recounted as his entries. In fact, the first story kicked off with the narrator finding his diary in the middle of an asteroid-hit crater. Occasionally, when Shonku has been indisposed, his neighbour, Avinash Babu, has written the entries in his diary.

MIA THERMOPOLIS

Mia a.k.a Amelia was a normal teenager, growing up in USA, when she realizes that she is actually the heir to the throne of a country called Genovia. Her diaries became *The Princess Diaries* (written by Meg Cabot), where she talks about her adventures of going from an American commoner to a European royal. The books have been very popular and also been made into a film (starring Anne Hathaway in the title role).

ROBINSON CRUSOE

The well-known story about a man who lands on an island after a shipwreck is narrated by himself as he goes about surviving in hostile territory and making friend and enemies. One of the earliest novels in English, Robinson Crusoe's story is very inspiring and is based on a real-life person (Alexander Selkirk) who was also shipwrecked and built a life for himself in a deserted island.

Can you re-write some of your favourite novels in diary form? What if the Harry Potter stories were written as diaries? Whose diary would you like them to be? Harry's? Ron Weasley's? Or somebody else's?

Hidden Treasure

In 'The Burmese Box', the box contains a whole lot of jewellery and gems, which the whole family is looking for.

Hidden treasure is one of the most enduring themes for children's books. Some of the most exciting stories have been around finding treasures hidden many years ago and then tracing it. There have been many clues, codes and maps . . . And somebody who solved the mystery!

Treasure Island (by Robert Louis Stevenson) is probably the most famous story about hidden treasure. As the name suggests, the treasure is located on a faraway island and a band of pirates start looking for it. There promises to be a lot of 'buried gold' shown on a map and marked with X (the traditional symbol to indicate treasure).

The narrator of the story is Jim Hawkins, a young boy who goes on the treasure hunt and is instrumental in finding the gold.

What fun would it be to stumble upon a coded map, full of directions to a secret hiding place! How would you go about cracking the code?

Is there a mystery in your family? Like Podi-pishi's Burmese box, is there any valuable item in your family that got misplaced and was never found? Are there any clues around it?

Child Detectives

Sherlock Holmes (created by Arthur Conan Doyle) and Hercule Poirot (created by Agatha Christie) are the two most famous detectives in fiction. But several authors have created very interesting child detectives as well.

Teenagers—some of whom operate in groups and some individually—have solved many interesting mysteries, gone on thrilling treasure hunts and chases.

The Famous Five

Created by Enid Blyton, The Famous Five is a group of four teenaged cousins (Julian, Dick, Anne and Georgina) and a dog (Timothy) who get involved in various mysterious happenings in the seaside town they spend their holidays in—including treasure hunting. They have been featured in twenty-one novels, many of which have been made into films, TV serials and cartoon series.

THE SECRET SEVEN

Another group of detectives created by the prolific Ms Blyton, Secret Seven Society is a group of seven fast friends (Peter, Janet, Barbara, Jack, George, Pam and Colin) who are also assisted by a dog (Scamper). These characters—like other similar ones— also took up mysteries in the neighbourhood and went about solving them.

NANCY DREW

The books featuring Nancy Drew were written by Carolyn Keene—this was actually a pseudonym for a collective of writers. A young girl of about eighteen, Nancy goes about in her own car and often in very exotic locations solving mysteries. Extremely popular, the stories in this series are still being written as Nancy Drew Files or Girl Detective, and even as graphic novels.

HARDY BOYS

The characters of Frank and Joe Hardy were created by the same collective of writers who created Nancy Drew, though the name used was Franklin W. Dixon. The two teenaged brothers often worked on cases of their father, who was also a detective. Mostly involved in adventure and action, the *Hardy Boys* series continued till very recently. A different version of the adventures has continued under the name *Undercover Brothers.*

Do you know of any Indian child detectives? Can you create one?

Would it be a single person or a group of friends? Will they be boys or girls? Where will they stay? How old will they be? What kind of mysteries will they solve? How will they look?

Other Goopys

The main character in the second story is called Goopy. There are two other similarly named characters, both of whom are quite famous.

Goopy Gyne, Bagha Byne

Written by Upendrakishore Roychoudhury, this is the story of a singer (Goopy Gyne literally means Goopy the Singer) and a drummer (Bagha Byne means Bagha the Drummer) who are granted three boons by the King of Ghosts. With the boons, they are able to play amazing music, get whatever food and clothes they want and go wherever they wish. An extremely popular story in Bengali, this was later made into a film by Satyajit Ray and the adventures of Goopy-Bagha are much loved even today.

Goofy

Mickey Mouse's second companion—other than Donald Duck. He is probably a dog (as his original name was Dippy Dawg) though this is not as popular as the facts that Mickey is a mouse and Donald is a duck! He is not very smart. In fact he's very clumsy, which lands him in many a trouble from which he has to be rescued by his friends.

Do you know of any more Goopy-s?